the Dublin Review

number ninety-three | WINTER 2023–24

GW00482603

EDITOR & PUBLISHER: BRENDAN BARRINGTON
DEPUTY PUBLISHER: AINGEALA FLANNERY

The Dublin Review, number ninety-three (Winter 2023–24).
Design by Atelier David Smith. Printed by Naas Printing Ltd.

ISBN 978-1-9196267-8-9

SUBMISSIONS: Please go to www.thedublinreview.com and follow the instructions on the 'Submissions' page. Although we encourage electronic submissions, we also accept physical submissions, to The Dublin Review, P.O. Box 7948, Dublin 1, Ireland. We cannot return physical manuscripts, so please do not send a unique or irreplaceable piece of work, and be sure to include your email address for a reply. *The Dublin Review* assumes no responsibility for unsolicited material.

SUBSCRIPTIONS: *The Dublin Review* is published quarterly. A subscription costs €34 / UK£26 per year in Ireland & Northern Ireland, €45 / UK£36 / US$60 per year for the rest of the world. Institutions add €15 / UK£13 / US$20. To subscribe or to order back issues, please use the secure-ordering facility at www.thedublinreview.com. Alternatively, you may send your address and a cheque or Visa/MC data and order details to Subscriptions, The Dublin Review, P.O. Box 7948, Dublin 1, Ireland. Credit-card orders are billed at the euro price. Please indicate if credit-card billing address differs from mailing address. If you have a question regarding an order, please email us at order@thedublinreview.com.

WEBSITE: www.thedublinreview.com

TRADE SALES: *The Dublin Review* is distributed to the trade by Gill & Macmillan Distribution, Hume Avenue, Park West, Dublin 12.

SALES REPRESENTATION: Robert Towers, 2 The Crescent, Monkstown, Co. Dublin, tel +353 1 2806532, fax +353 1 2806020.

The Dublin Review receives financial assistance from the Arts Council.

Contents | *number ninety-three* | WINTER 2023–24

Ransom

ROISIN AGNEW

The building didn't have a lift: that was how Rebecca could afford to live there. She and Jo lived on the top floor, the ninth. On the seventh there was an actress in her sixties, who Jo assured Rebecca had been a pretty big TV star in her day. The actress liked to be watched. From the stairwell, on your way up or down, you could often see her through the open door, walking around the apartment on the phone, smoking, in a loose house dress, two hungry cats weaving their way behind her like dolphins in the wake of a ship. The actress was the first thing that had made Rebecca feel she was far from home. She was a good person, the actress. She often came to check on Jo and never complained about the smell.

That morning, though, there was no sign of the actress. Rebecca pushed her way into the apartment and made her way to the kitchen, noticing that Jo's bedroom door was closed. She turned on a podcast and loudly started to unpack the groceries. When everything was in its place, she pulled a tiny chair to the tiny kitchen table and took out an oil bun from a large brown paper bag. Now that she wasn't drinking she ate oil buns constantly.

She opened her laptop and began to reread the email.

> Reba,
>
> How are you? You've moved to That City Fi tells me? I saw her last week on the street, we're neighbours now! I thought it was beautiful when I went there last summer.

Two pigeons landed unseen on the roof above, cooing coyly at each other. 'Horny,' Rebecca said quietly.

The apartment had sloping ceilings and skylights that filled the space with blinding light on sunny days. It was painted white and the floorboards were chipping. From the entrance hall, doors on the left led to Rebecca's room, the bathroom, and Jo's room, while to the right there was a small sitting room and, after that, a little corridor that ended in french windows protected by low iron bars that looked across to a ministerial building. Rebecca had once waited in that building for two hours before being told she was in the wrong place.

At the end of the flat was the kitchen, long and narrow. It had two small porthole windows on either end, and if you got on your toes you could see over the orange rooftops to the sea, which was actually a river.

Rebecca pulled out another bun and kept reading.

> No doubt you're aware of what's happened between me and Laura and that things have now ended up in family court. My lawyer suggested I reach out to a previous partner, and of course I thought of you. I feel I have to fill you in on some of the details in order for you to make an informed decision.

A door opened and there was Jo in an old T-shirt and underwear. Her head was shaved and the bags under her eyes were an aubergine purple. She was small-breasted and thick around the thighs and Rebecca found her sexy even though she was not her type. The few times Jo and Rebecca walked around the neighbourhood together, people always looked at Rebecca and not Jo. Men liked women to look like women in The City.

'Reba,' Jo almost choked. She rubbed her eyes and squinted through the sunlight.

'Good afternoon!' Rebecca said. She felt large and goofy. She turned the radio off.

'I'm so sorry ... I said I'd go to the market with you ...'

Jo made an exaggerated sad face. She had an American accent but the catarrhal Rs placed her as native of The City.

'Don't worry. It's good for me to get lost. Where's our guy?'

Jo turned back into the darkness of the room and started making sounds at something. 'Fofo! Fofo!' There was a scratching over floorboards and a long-haired yellow dog with bat ears and a pink nose came out of the bedroom. He looked up at Jo and shuddered.

'Meco! Meco!' Rebecca whispered, clicking her tongue at him.

He was like a baby kangaroo, Rebecca thought. Meco, Jo had told her, was the name of her favourite nudist beach. This was a silly name, Rebecca thought, since its chief purpose seemed to be to inform strangers that you frequented nudist beaches.

'Fofofofofofofo,' Jo said, roughing the dog up gently, grabbing his muzzle and kissing it.

'I have to go to work today as well. Last minute,' Jo said with an exhausted sigh. Jo worked in a cocktail bar in a hotel.

'Yeah I went to a little thing, not even a party. I would have told you but it was shit to be honest, pff.'

'All good. I was at dinner with P and Chiara.'

Rebecca would've liked to have gone to that party. P and Chiara had a baby.

Jo went over to Meco and emptied the expensive dog food into his bowl before padding into the bathroom.

Rebecca returned to the oil buns as the shower began to run. She looked at Meco. While he was here everything was OK. When he disappeared down the little hall was when you had to start worrying. Rebecca returned to the email.

As incriminating as any plea of innocence might sound these days, circumstances force me to make one to you.

She wondered again about the thrill of seeing his name in her inbox. She skipped to the end.

> I'm very sorry I have to ask this favour of you, as you can imagine.
>
> Let me know your thoughts and if you would like to talk on the phone about it.
>
> Love, Nick

The smell hit her then. Meco crept back from behind the corner to lie under the table in the hall, a bashful look on his face. She got up before she could get annoyed, lit some incense, and left the apartment shouting that she would see Jo later.

The street below was crowded and heat rose from the cobblestones like exhaust. The sun was high. The man from the souvenir shop gave Rebecca a big smile and a wave as she crossed the street. He was always leaning against the entrance and in high spirits, arguing with his wife and daughter behind him, who were always out of sight. He'd asked her about herself after the third time she went into his shop, and had in turn offered information. He was from Dhaka, had been living in The City for fifteen years, and his opinion of the local people was final. 'Lazy lazy lazy,' he'd said.

She decided to make her way to a bar known as The Cat, which was a good walk, forty minutes. They gave her free Coca-Colas at The Cat sometimes, possibly because she was often on her own. She decided she would take the coastal route and turned left onto the steep limestone steps that climbed to the next level of the city. Orange trees gave the air a deep floral fragrance rounded with citrus notes. The orange blossom would cling to the hot air all day and then curl into everything in the coolness of the night.

At the top of the stairs there was a square, the art school standing in one corner surrounded by mopeds and scantily dressed golden-brown students. Jacaranda trees dotted the perimeter of the square. They had no smell, the jacarandas, but huge exuberant bursts of tiny purple flowers. When you looked at things from a height, the jacaranda trees formed long purple veins through the city. From the square Rebecca would descend and walk towards the docks, she decided, between the tram tracks and the sea.

The City's giant bridge became visible, steel rising out of the sweltering air like a mirage, rusting and monstrous. Walking between the docks and the tram tracks, Rebecca thought how she'd always liked ports and shipping containers, the labour taking place on a public stage. She could smell diesel and the coldness of the sea. Someone was frying fish nearby.

She was going to have to do something about Jo. Rebecca had first made contact with her months ago, before she'd moved to The City, finding her on a website that Chiara had recommended. The apartment looked impossibly beautiful in the listing. As soon as she'd started emailing, Jo had said that she'd read Rebecca's magazine, owned three editions, and that she wanted to give Rebecca the bigger room but at the same price. The piñata of life had split open right above Rebecca's head and it was raining down on her.

Jo had insisted on picking Rebecca up at the airport – and there she had been, shaved head, branded shell jacket and jeans, effortlessly something. Jo had given her a tentative hug, saying it was great to finally meet in person, then disappeared to get the car, leaving Rebecca to take in the warmth of the sun in the smoking area. After fifteen minutes driving, Jo had told Rebecca that she'd just been released from a psychiatric ward and was heavily sedated, but that she could still drive. 'What you write about and where you're from,' Jo had said, 'I can tell I can talk to you about these things and that you won't judge me. Here it's not like that.' Rebecca told Jo it was fine, not to worry, she'd lived with two bipolar girls for many years and she was accustomed to having friends with varying degrees of mental health issues. She had some problems herself, it was OK.

When they arrived at the apartment a few minutes later it was even better than Rebecca had expected, like an American film set in Europe, with a balance of shabbiness and natural lighting so perfect it seemed almost artificial. Then there was the dog. Rebecca had seen photos and even a video of him but now she couldn't stop looking at Meco: small, with scruffy yellowish hair and giant pink ears. 'Like a rabbit crossed with an Irish wolfhound,' as she had put it to her mother on the phone. On first approach he'd retreated, ears back but wagging his tail, which made it look like he was squirming away. Eventually, Meco had allowed some petting, then a belly scratch. He was inseparable from Jo, devoted, and went berserk with adoration when she riled him up with funny voices.

Rebecca had noticed the smell right away, and asked Jo about it. Jo explained that she had recently picked up Meco from her mother and stepfather's house in the countryside, where he had been staying while she had been hospitalized. He'd just been in the house a few days and was still getting used to it. 'He doesn't like it outside,' Jo had said.

That first night Jo brought Rebecca out to a bar that was off the tourist circuit, full of old men and only one brand of beer that cost as much as a pack of chewing gum cost at home. Jo told Rebecca about the comforting experience of fucking a German boy who didn't care for her in the same way she didn't care for him, about her stepdad's nauseating coddling, and about the last job she'd had before her breakdown. Rebecca felt sorry for her despite the tired coolness with which she delivered all this.

Jo generally didn't rise until early afternoon, groggy from medication and almost unable to speak. She would sit in her pyjamas eating biscuits out of a large bag at the tiny kitchen table while watching reruns of *Friends*. She barely left the house except to go to work, and the only person who ever called around was the actress. Jo would always know it was her and be at the door by the time Rebecca had poked her head out of her bedroom door. The actress would be there in an airy dress holding on to Jo's hand, her face like a Grecian mask frozen in an expression of profound concern. The first time this happened, Rebecca had said hello in the other language and walked with her outstretched hand towards the actress in the doorway. At this, Jo had turned to look at her with an expression of almost savage indignation that froze Rebecca in her tracks. Maybe she'd missed something because of the language barrier. But the actress had simply smiled, her face caving into an expression of goodwill that made Rebecca instantly like her, and when Rebecca glanced back at Jo she had settled into her usual languid half-smile.

As the weeks went by it became clear to Rebecca that Jo was never going to take Meco outside. He was settling in, he was scared of the outdoors, she didn't want to traumatize him, she'd take him when he was ready. Then she'd started to just outright lie: 'It's dangerous on our street … he could be run over … I did take him out just for a second, he didn't like it …' When Rebecca offered to take him out and house-train him, Jo had looked at her dead on and widened her eyes. 'I don't want anyone taking Meco outside the house, yes?'

By the time Jo woke up each day, Meco would've urinated three times and defecated at least once. If he got a fright he would shit more. Rebecca started putting newspapers down for him in the spot he liked to use, but often she would come home from her endless mornings in the library and Jo would've thrown the newspapers out without replacing them.

The floorboards where Meco shat and pissed began to stain and no amount of scrubbing would get it out. Rebecca's searches online suggested white wine vinegar, and while it helped with the stains, it also insinuated itself into all the other smells and flavours in the apartment. No matter what she did or where she was, the smell of vinegar and dog shit was perceptible on the periphery of her senses. Once, in the shower, the smell overpowered her so entirely that she turned the taps off, convinced it was coming through the pipes and that she was scrubbing it into herself.

But the worst came when she realized you could smell it all the way down to the seventh floor. After that, she went to the Bangladeshi man's shop and bought four cylinders of incense and started to hide in her room.

*

The Cat wasn't full: it was still relatively early. Rebecca's thoughts had made her walk quickly, and sunset was still less than an hour away, which meant the terrace would be uncomfortably hot.

She smiled and said hello to the two waiters who recognized her, the boss waiter and the young waiter, both wearing white shirts and dress trousers. The Cat was in the neighbourhood where most of the embassies and consulates had their headquarters, along with some of the national museums, and the sense of drowsiness The City emanated seemed to intensify in its vicinity.

Behind the mirrored bar a woman with a giant crop of curly hair was mixing drinks and looking at Rebecca with curiosity as she jiggled up and down. Even the unattractive people were attractive here, Rebecca thought. She took a seat in the shade of the bar that looked over the terrace and watched the two men. At the table closest to Rebecca's there was an elderly couple and a little boy. All three were dressed in expensive linens and cottons cut in the cleanest ways. Grandmother and Grandfather were around seventy-five, Rebecca guessed, with hairdos and perfect teeth that seemed almost unnatural. Little whiffs of cologne came her way every time Grandfather moved. Grandmother wore a pair of glasses that looked like she'd had them since the 1960s and her hair was dyed blonde in the way white hair is dyed blonde. The little boy was clearly not going to be an annoying child to sit next to. He was soft-looking and pudgy, happy to be in that bar with his grandparents. Someone had dressed him up for the benefit of the grandparents and the grandparents had dressed themselves up for the benefit of someone.

Rebecca was going to have a drink. She would have the first drink she'd had since moving to The City. A change of setting had been helpful. It had been very helpful! This was a hiccup. She blamed Nick's email. She would have one drink, Rebecca said to herself, and she would start looking for a new place to live. After that, she would think about the character reference or whatever it was Nick had asked of her. She ordered the standard dry white wine you ordered and hoped that the young waiter would come over and flirt with her, which he did.

When she got home, it took a moment for her to understand what had happened. The entrance hall was always bare, aside from an antique ladder propped up against one wall with creepers running down it. It was only after she'd dropped her things in her bedroom and come back into the hall that she finally noticed: all the furniture had disappeared. She went from room to room. Chairs, prints, lamps, vases, cushions, plants, carpets, the TV, the tiny table and the tiny chairs in the kitchen – all gone. The whole apartment aside from her bedroom was bare, with the exception of the couch, which oddly remained. For a second Rebecca was scared the thief was still there. But then there was a muffled 'Fofo' from Jo's bedroom, some excited scratching, and Jo came out trailed by Meco. She walked past Rebecca as though she wasn't there and slammed the bathroom door behind her. The slam upset Meco and for a second he walked in half circles, whimpering. Rebecca let out a long sigh and went into the kitchen. When the bathroom door opened her voice came out with a boom.

'Jo!'

Jo stopped dead and looked at Rebecca. Her white shirt and smart black trousers looked good on her. She smiled and shrugged her shoulders as though Rebecca was a particularly tedious child who was failing to grasp the lesson again.

'Reba,' she coughed. 'We can talk tomorrow, I'm late.'

'Where is all the furniture, Jo?'

Jo scrunched her face and cocked her head in mock bemusement.

'Why does that matter to you? It's my furniture.'

'That's a reasonable, adult answer! Where is it?'

Without thinking she rushed across the kitchen and pushed the door to

Jo's room open. Piled to the ceiling, leaving nothing but a tiny path to the bed, was all of the furniture. Rebecca gasped. Then she started laughing.

'What the fuck. What the fuck. Why?'

'You have no respect, you are just … here!' Jo snarled.

'What the fuck are you talking about?'

Jo suddenly darted forward, coming up so close to Rebecca's face that she could smell the cigarettes and malty biscuits on her breath.

'Today! I go into the bathroom. And at the bottom of the toilet there is some of your blood.'

'What?'

'In the toilet. Your menstrual blood. It's nasty.'

Rebecca was scared. She had never hit anyone, except an ex-boyfriend once. She started pacing the kitchen.

'Look. Give me my deposit back and I'll be gone tonight. I promise you.'

'I don't have it,' Jo replied flatly, walking into her room and starting to put things in a bag.

Rebecca kept pacing trying to get her breath back.

'I know, but when you have time tonight, transfer it to me. Maybe take a screengrab and send me the photo.'

'It's not there.'

'What do you mean?'

'It's not in my account.'

'Where is it?'

'I had people I needed to pay.' Jo put her jacket on, picked up her bag, and looked at Rebecca with leering contempt. 'I'll call my stepdad on my way to work and see what we can do.'

'OK. I won't start packing until I hear from you.'

Jo offered her face to Meco, letting him lick her lips, before leaving the flat without replying.

Rebecca was trembling. She didn't know what she was going to do. She got a beer out of the fridge and texted Chiara a vague but urgent-sounding message about the possibility of staying the night, things having gone wrong. She went into her room and got on all fours to retrieve the suitcases from under her bed. Her phone vibrated: a text from Jo.

'I'm keeping the deposit. That is how it works. You have been here 5 weeks. You have to leave my apartment now.'

Rebecca thought for a second, then rang Jo. It rang out. She rang again. Same. She sat down on the bed that was covered in a beautiful multi-coloured throw she had bought. There was a scratching sound and Meco's nose poked its way through the gap in the door. Rebecca had forgotten about him. 'Fofo! Fofo!' He trotted over to her and she grabbed his face with both hands and blew kisses at him. He was a real sweetheart and deserved better, Rebecca thought. They both did.

The benches in that part of the park were placed in a circular formation around a single enormous tree whose boughs and branches formed a thick flowerless canopy that covered the whole area. A mishmash of iron trellises buckled beneath its girth, evidently built at different times to meet the insatiable demands of the tree's expansion. Nineteenth-century lamps ran along the back of the benches, dropping gentle pools of gold that moths and confused bumblebees flitted through. Old men, teenage couples, and other people who didn't want to be well lit sat on this side of the park. Rebecca sat on a bench, balancing a cup of beer between her thighs and trying to get Meco to sit.

The dog had calmed down finally, and now stood at attention, giant bat ears alert, his lithe body darting at every movement then squirming away in fright. He was having a good time.

She had acted with focus and determination, dropping all her stuff at Chiara's before going back to pick up Meco. The plan had been to head straight for the park. But as she'd locked the apartment door and made her way down the marble steps, she'd come face to face with the actress on her landing. The actress was locking her door and dressed to go out, a botanical musk rising from the deep cleavage of her breasts as she jingled her hands around the door handle. She looked marvellous, like Sofia Loren if Sofia Loren had been born a parrot, Rebecca thought. After collecting herself, Rebecca had made a two-toned 'Ahhh!' to indicate to the actress that she looked very nice. The actress smiled, holding the smile a second too long, as though someone might take a photo, then linked arms with Rebecca while saying something to the effect that she needed help in those shoes. Rebecca, half-dazzled by the unexpected obstacle and the green chiffon dress, supported the actress down the seven flights of stairs and attempted to leave her with the understanding that she was bringing the dog to an emergency vet appointment.

Out on the street, the actress jingled a kiss at Rebecca, thanked her, and crossed the road after looking left and right. Rebecca turned to find Meco flat on the pavement in a state of terror, ears back, whimpering. She tried to cajole him up, but his whimpers only became louder and more pathetic. Eventually she called the souvenir shop owner to the entrance and asked him if he would sell her some dog treats. The snacks did the trick, distracting Meco away from the Saturday-night crowds. The Bangladeshi man had stayed in his shop entrance laughing at the scene, waving Rebecca off into the night with a gesture that looked almost like a blessing.

Now, settled in the park, encased in benign lumbering gloom, Rebecca renewed her efforts to get Meco to sit. He finally sat and she attempted a photo in selfie mode. The flash came on, blinding Rebecca, who involuntarily exclaimed a disgusted 'Oh!'. Her bench neighbours, two old men, let out a gummy laugh in her direction. They must think she was a lonely, drunk tourist taking selfies with her pet, she thought. Well, she wasn't! She lived here, and this wasn't her pet, and she had a plan.

Rebecca took another sip and another selfie, this time making sure the flash was off. She then looked at her handiwork. In the one with the flash, Meco looked like he'd seen a ghost while in an air tunnel, and Rebecca had five chins. In the second, Rebecca looked very drunk and all you saw of Meco were his kangaroo ears and glinting night eyes. She took another. In this one she looked like she was posing for something and Meco looked, ironically, constipated. She gulped her beer and sent that last one to Jo: '2 months deposit back.'

On the far side of the park, yellow festoon lights hung among the trees and cigarette smoke snaked through the air above a sea of tables full of young families and well-dressed couples. Children ran through the trellises and climbed up the ancient tree in the dark, shrieking. Meco looked at them, hopping from one leg to another, seemingly torn between a desire to follow them and to hide from them. 'I feel you,' Rebecca mumbled. She looked at the tree again and then typed into her phone. It was a cedar! She'd looked it up, and found a series of photos of the tree through the years. Two children came to pet Meco gingerly, whispering deafeningly at each other as he trembled under their hands. Her phone vibrated.

'What the fuck???? Where are you?'

Rebecca mashed at her phone. 'Give me back my deposit Jo.'

'What are you doing Rebecca!!!?'

'I've taken the dog and you won't get him back until I have my deposit.' Then she added, 'Sorry', and immediately regretted it.

She wondered if she could go to jail for kidnapping Meco and looked it up. She could. That would at least get her out of writing a character reference for Nick. No family court hearing over child custody could take seriously a character reference written by a dog thief. It was for the best, really, all in all. She'd go to jail, Nick would be forced to take responsibility for the thing he had probably done, and Meco would end up in a dog home or with nicer people. It would all be good.

The phone vibrated. 'Where are you???? I can get off in 20 minutes.'

Rebecca replied, 'I don't care. I want my deposit back. Send me that and then we talk.' It was starting to sound vaguely ridiculous. She went over to the kiosk to order another beer.

She wondered if she'd done the right thing. Had she kidnapped the dog of a mentally ill person over money?

But they owed her – in one way or another they owed her. Jo owed her two months' rent. And Nick owed her. How much did character references go for these days? Rebecca got out her phone. Jo would be a while yet.

Dear Nick,

How nice to hear from you despite the circumstances ...

The leash tugged in her hand and she looked up. Meco was squatting over a flower bed, an expression of guilt and relief spreading across his whiskered face.

The ascent of Stromboli

NICK HOLDSTOCK

1

For the first hour I was only walking along an Italian hillside, glancing at the sea, watching for lizards, wishing there was shade. The explosion stopped me. It was not unlike thunder. But the sky was blue and of course I knew the volcano on Stromboli was active, I *wanted* it to be active. Ten minutes later there was another explosion. A brown plume rose from the summit. Soon I passed a sign warning me not to take a higher path without a guide. Since two violent major explosions in 2019, during which lava flowed towards inhabited areas and the shock waves broke windows, four hundred metres of elevation has been the legal limit for climbers, even if accompanied by a guide. In San Vincenzo, the island's main port, you are never far from a sign directing people to the nearest assembly area in the event of a tsunami. Yet despite these reminders of the destructive power of plate tectonics, the mood all over the island – in the small lanes, in the cafés, on the black sand beaches – appeared entirely without fear. The most obvious source of danger seemed to be the miniature three-wheeled trucks that barrelled along the narrow roads with an urgency suggesting some great crisis.

After two hours' walking I reached the edge of the Sciara del Fuoco, a blackened slope that extends downward from the crater to the sea. It was 5 p.m., several hours before the guided groups would arrive, and so I took a prohibited path to a higher viewing spot. There I sat alone and kept my gaze on a single point in space for the next two hours. The explosions increased in frequency until they were occurring every ten minutes. There was white smoke. Grey smoke. My neck began to hurt from being perpetually tilted back. The knowledge that I shouldn't have been in that place without a guide was exciting, but also distracting. I wanted to focus all of my consciousness on the crater, but I found myself mentally justifying my actions to the authority figure I was sure would arrive soon. The roughly one hundred metres that I had illegally climbed were no more treacherous than the rest of the path, I said to this figure. And if the volcano suddenly threw superheated rocks in my direction, no guide could protect me. The escape routes, in any event, were obvious. If burning death did start to fall from the sky, no one would need to be told to leave.

A voice of reason countered these arguments by suggesting that the requirement for a guide was as much about keeping the island economically sustainable as it was about safety. Since the guides were no longer allowed to take people to the crater, there had to be some way to justify their existence. Only the worst kind of miserly, over-privileged tourist would begrudge spending twenty-five euros for the chance to have a marginally better view of a spectacular natural sight while helping support the local community. But having come this far, I did not want to give up my position.

Only when I saw a few people approaching from below did I retreat to the lower, legal observation point at 290 metres. The explosions began to throw up rocks. The smoke got darker. A French man with a large rucksack appeared. An Italian couple followed. The initial burst of magma against the darkening sky was wonderful and terrifying. The French man reached into his rucksack and brought out a metal object with great care. He spread a white cloth on the ground as if preparing for the most important picnic of his life. He placed the object on the cloth, then looked around with pride. When the drone lifted into the air I hated its electric mosquito noise. As it rose the collective wonder at the growing explosions was transferred to the small whining object that was going where we could not. Yet I too clustered round the 4K screen with a sense of amazement. Being able to see the new level of detail increased my awe yet also seemed to slightly devalue what the naked eye had found incredible only moments ago. It made me need to get closer.

At sunset the guided groups approached. They wore miner's helmets and as I watched them ascend to the higher vantage point I wished I was going with them. The detonations had become more frequent. Sometimes there was smoke but no sound of an explosion. Sometimes there was smoke, then an explosion, then a crimson leap of magma. The unpredictability of this sequence made it seem as if causation had been unsettled, sound and light free to pick the order in which they were perceptible. In the dark the magma was a self-illuminating spray that showered the rim of the crater. Between the visible explosions a reddish glow played around the summit. It got cold. I was very thirsty. The shortest way down was not the path I had taken. I did not want to have to navigate an unknown path in the darkness with only the wan light of a torch whose batteries had been in there for five years. I told myself I would leave after the next big explosion. But as soon as that occurred I had to wait for the next one.

A long line of lights began to descend towards us. The group came down quickly, then our darkness and quiet were gone as they streamed past talking of dinner, a needy friend, how much they liked Milan. I walked back and forth trying to warm up, my neck painful from the hours attending to the rim of the crater. I was waiting for a gigantic explosion, an event I knew was improbable, given the volcano's moderate recent seismic history. Still, the fear of missing some greater proof of what had already been established kept me up there, shivering, anxious about getting back down. I thought of a recent paper in *Nature* about Stromboli, which had spoken of the explosive consequences of the mingling of a 'hotter, volatile rich and primitive magma type' with 'a cooler, degassed and more evolved end-member'. After the obligatory caveats, and dispassionate equivocation, the paper concluded that recent data 'could warn a new eruptive cycle has opened'. In my eagerness for this to be true I dismissed this 'could' as being for form's sake. Never mind the consequences for the people of the island, the potential loss of life and impoverishment: I wanted huge detonations, lava flow, the sky more red than black.

I cannot plead a lifelong fascination with volcanoes. A child doing a school project probably knows more than me about how they work. But last year I watched a film in which Stromboli briefly featured. From that moment it became important for me to observe a volcano erupting at some point in my life. I suspect this kind of sudden, erratic urge is one of the gifts – or symptoms – of reaching middle age.

Soon I was the only person left at the observation post. There were no more lights above. I watched the volcano maintain the same remarkable yet unsatisfactory level of activity. I put on more clothes. I walked back and forth, did little jumps, told myself it wasn't really cold. If I wasn't willing to endure a bit of shivering, I didn't deserve to see a paroxysm of lava.

2

There are several paths that lead to the crater of Stromboli. On the morning I first arrived on the island I had scouted a path that started only ten minutes from a shopping street. The path was overgrown and steep, I had no water and was wearing too many clothes, and yet I started upwards while saying out loud, 'You are not doing this.' I continued upwards for five minutes then obeyed my own command.

The morning after staying on the volcano I remembered that path. In the clarity of Google Earth it seemed far more plausible. The first three hundred metres were just a straight line through verdant green. Apart from an obser-vatory run by the University of Florence, there were no other structures along the way. As I zoomed in on the white building it assumed the status of a sentry house, but if I could pass it without being stopped then I could keep going until the vegetation ended. At that point the green was replaced by the brownish grey of a lunar surface. The path swung left then turned sharply right towards the crater, and while this had to mean an ascent of five hundred metres, the lack of visible clues to the gradient meant that my eyes were undaunted. They followed the reassuring line onscreen until they met the caption 'Portella di Stromboli'. Once I passed through there – I could not help imagining an actual gateway – I would enter the Valle della Luna that ran along the crater. The image showed smoke hovering over the crater.

I spent a long time staring at these images. The thought of being up there alone was frightening, but it had the insane appeal of standing on another planet. I wasn't sure it would be possible. There might be locked gates. Fences. Barbed wire. Even if there weren't, the little I'd seen of the real path suggested it would be a scramble through thick overgrowth.

An hour later I was headed for the path with a rucksack full of water. If they stopped me, so be it. I felt I had to try. As I passed the last few houses I expected to be stopped and challenged about my intentions. I was ready to deny them completely. *I am just walking*, I would say. *I don't know where I'm going.*

At 10 a.m. it was already hot. I pushed up through the vegetation, stumbling and sliding. One moment the narrow path was on solid ground, the next it was a wide crack full of loose dirt and stones. There was no need to hurry; I hurried. I was impatient to reach the crater and fearful of being stopped. Soon there would be another sign telling me that I had reached the permissible elevation. I didn't want to see this sign, but if it was there, I couldn't wait to see it.

I was passing through an area of burnt trees when bells began to toll. At first I heard them as a condemnation of what I was doing, then as a tocsin of warning. What could be a greater cliché than the foreign tourist who perishes because he thinks he knows best? I contemplated going back down. I remembered it was Sunday, the bells were ringing for Mass. I kept going.

Soon the ground became softer, partly ash, far harder to climb. Above me I saw the end of the vegetation and the start of the grey zone. I was sure that if there were going to be any barriers or signs warning me not to go further, they would be placed at that point. It was their last chance to stop me.

Even as I made slower progress on the steepening slope, I tried to go faster. I thought of how my orange rucksack must be highly visible from the town. People would say, 'What is that idiot doing?' When I came down they would be waiting. There would be shouting, arguments, unsmiling police.

I reached the grey zone. There were no warning signs. No fences. Either no one cared, or they thought no one would be stupid enough to make the climb. I sat on a rock. I drank water. Without vegetation I felt very exposed on the side of the volcano. I realized there were two paths ahead, one that went around the volcano, another that zigzagged up. The latter wasn't shown on Google Earth. Neither was really a path – just some foot-disturbed ash. They indicated a direction of travel but did nothing to facilitate movement. The one going straight up seemed an easier climb, but I rejected it. It wasn't the one I'd imagined doing.

I started. Each step in the ash raised dust. As I carefully placed my feet, and then watched them slide down, for the first time I fully comprehended that there was now nothing to stop me going up to the Door of Stromboli, then the Valley of the Moon, all the way to the crater. I had plenty of water. It was only 11 a.m. After I had gone round the volcano a little further there would be a difficult ascent on sandy ash, but I believed I was capable of making the climb.

The prospect of being up there, on my own, unbeknownst to anyone, was suddenly terrifying. It was as if the minor fear of being stopped had been blocking my vision for hours but now had suddenly stepped aside to reveal this greater dread. I'd seen that lunar area on Google Maps, in all its otherworldliness, and this made it far more terrifying than if it had been unknown.

And yet, I had not started climbing with the goal of only reaching halfway. The risk was probably no greater than what I had faced climbing mountains of similar height elsewhere, where injury and death, in the absence of any assistance, had been just as plausible. I had been scared in many of those situations, I had often had to force myself to go on, but after the worst was over, when I had reached a point of safety, the sense not just of relief, but also of achievement at overcoming my fear, was more powerful than anything else I would feel in my ordinary life for weeks, months. This ascent, if completed, would be something I would be proud of for many years, perhaps the rest of my life. The satisfaction of overcoming my fear would be a small, bright episode I could always replay.

I began my descent.

Pool pump

JESS RAYMON

Six months ago, someone attempted to kill me. Before that, all I had to worry about was my above-ground swimming pool business and keeping Josie happy. The trial of my assailant is next week. I'm so anxious that I'm reading a list of steps for building my love muscle.

At first, surviving the attack flooded me with confidence. I needed only a few hours of sleep at night. I could deadlift three hundred pounds – double what I could before. All the DIY work I'd been putting off for a decade – clearing oil cans from the yard, pruning back the rhubarb – was done in a week. And that rhubarb was frozen solid. Once you've grabbed the barrel of a loaded shotgun with bare hands, such tasks are nothing.

Before long, I stopped needing sleep altogether. I started seeing things, hearing things. I could perceive the moonlight vibrating on the tops of my eyelids; without looking out the window I could tell if the moon was full or crescent, the sky cloudy or clear. My senses grew so loud I could taste the neighbour's pork cutlets sizzling in the oven, down to the honey-mustard sauce; I could hear the newborn crying from all the way past the meth house. Neighbourhood watch is one thing, but when the dealer's dog's bark courses through your eardrums and you have a torrent of confidence in your blood, you run into problems. I don't blame Josie for leaving me, I really don't. I just want her back home.

You have to build love muscle. It won't grow on its own. Step one is refocusing your thoughts away from regret and self-loathing, to memories that make you happy. Josie made me happy. Last year in the dead of summer, she polished off an entire bottle of blue curaçao, fell into my lap, and whispered into my ear that my heart was like a pool pump. I snapped her bra strap and made to push her off me. She was violent when she drank sweet liquors. But she wrapped her arms around me and whispered, 'No, baby, I mean stable. Like the plastic valves you're always talking about. Predictable. I know exactly what you're made of.'

Not long after she said this to me, I did a pool set-up job for a young musclehead guy up Fork Road, deep in the woods. He said he didn't want any slime in his pool. He said he wanted to see a whirlpool moving the water around in circles. Against my better judgement, I installed a bigger pump than I normally would. I told him that with all the bugs up there he had to keep the pool clean. He called me back up a couple weeks later. I smelled the septic fishy smell before I even looked in the pool. I took apart the pump, and when I popped the plastic valve out, a heap of meaty horseflies fell into my hand. One fly started buzzing, a zombie.

I told Josie that story. She laughed. Any time I was too quiet, she would put her ear to my chest and make a buzzing noise, say my filter was clogged with zombie flies.

A little while after she moved in, I was making room in the shed for a new lawnmower and I found a duffel bag. It wasn't mine. The top flap wasn't zipped and I could see a long leather strap with a hot-pink tassel. I was curious, as any man would be. I unzipped a bit, saw whips, plastic dildos. I pulled out a nipple clamp and this string of big pearls. I didn't know what half of those things were used for. I took the duffel bag inside and placed it on the kitchen table. The bag disappeared, but a few nights later Josie sat on the edge of the bed and told me her ex used to make her do things. Things she didn't want to like. Those were her exact words. I was baffled. Her ex was a woman. Women don't abuse women. They understand each other's feelings. When I said this she rolled her eyes. Said that if you know what someone's feeling, it only makes it easier to manipulate them.

We started going to Mr Chicken every Sunday. As we sat in my truck eating, there'd be a flash of light from outside, then dark, then light again.

Someone was flashing their headlights at us. After the third time it happened, Josie told me it was her ex's truck. I drove us down to the police station and tried to press charges. The cops went away to check their computer, came back and told us the truck was registered to a woman. Yes, I told them, that's her ex. The cop laughed, scratched his moustache and said women don't stalk women to intimidate them, it's probably nothing to be worried about. He said we were wasting police time.

Less than a month later, in the early hours of the morning, an intruder broke into our house. I heard a lamp crash in the TV room, I felt something click in my neck. My body flooded with adrenaline and I swear I could smell the Mr Chicken Cajun burger. I grabbed a rifle from the bottom of the wardrobe. You know what was going through my head in that moment? Nothing. Not one single thought. I was fully present. I heard the floor creaks move further away, into the kitchen. Under the dim blue light, I peered in from behind the fridge. I could tell it was Josie's ex: she has no neck and a conical head. A balaclava doesn't change that. When she turned her shotgun in my direction, I ripped the door off the pasta cupboard and swung at her head. Only survival was on my mind. The cupboard handle caught the chain around her neck, and I remember the way it rattled when it hit the linoleum.

After the break-in, I have little recollection of Josie's presence in our house. The only thing I remember was one afternoon, when she went out to the shed and came back with a bungee cord. She asked me to tie her up. I said no. Good thing, too. She slapped me across the face, then laughed, and then pulled me to her and kissed me on the lips. She told me she was just testing me, making sure my heart was still made of the plastic valves she knows and trusts. I apologized for the way I'd been acting, and she said it was fine. But she stopped speaking to me. She would sit in the dark on the edge of the bed, perfectly still, face lit up by a white screen. Her muscles would be clenched, her breath was deep and heavy as she typed back quickly, with both fingers. She said she was talking to her sister.

Around that time, the dealer started letting his dog out at night on its own. One night, as a gesture, I bought Josie the sour dinosaur chews she likes and put on *Cops*. She ate a red stegosaurus and glanced at the TV as the music grew tense, but then went back to her phone. The dog started barking – loud and rusty sounds that seemed to scratch the inside of my skull. A muscle twitched behind my right ear, a man got shot on TV, and I was out the door. Shirtless. Dead of winter and I didn't feel a thing. Josie called after me.

When I came up for air, my hands were numb from cold and covered in fur and blood. A still-warm mass in my lap, wailing out in pain. Half dead, half alive.

Be compassionate when shit hits the fan. I think that's the best sentence in the love-muscle article. Josie ended up showing compassion to the dog. I felt her hand on my shoulder, smelled her breath sweet from the sour dinosaur chews. The dog let out another wail and Josie said, 'What the fuck are you doing, the dog is in pain, you know whose dog this is, he's gonna hear it, fucking finish it.' She ran into the house, and reappeared with the sharpest kitchen knife. She muttered 'coward' under her breath as she ran that knife into the dog's neck. She didn't want to see me in trouble with the dealer, she didn't want to see the dog in pain. You can meditate for years at the top of a mountain wishing for world peace: that's not compassion. What Josie did took compassion.

After the dog, she stopped speaking to me. Occasionally she'd come home with oddities – Black Forest cake or duck eggs – but she never put them in the fridge or ate them. They would sit on the counter rotting. And she started showering. Before she'd only ever taken baths or swam in the pool.

Every night I lay awake, sweat steaming through my pores, watching Josie's ribcage twitch as she sighed in her sleep. I wanted to make it right, but I didn't know how. One night I must have dozed off for half an hour. When I woke she wasn't there. That was eleven weeks ago. The last I've seen her. I haven't washed our sheets.

Things grew darker alone. Every now and then I'd hear the dog barking, knowing full well it was dead. I got so anxious I tried the 'self-love sucker punch'. I took deep breaths and envisioned the future I wanted as now. When I dozed off, I saw Josie, hair stringy from the pool, wearing her watermelon-print camisole. It's summer, the grass is warm, and the dragonflies are buzzing. She's reading the local paper in her lawn chair. There's something on her skin, little charcoal smudges. I make to rub it off her collarbone, but she recoils from my touch and points towards the pool. It's perfectly still. Nothing is moving, and I'm wondering how the pump is shot already. Then I notice the water's surface is covered in black oil, and my reflection is distorted, I can't see myself clearly, and when I look back for Josie, the camisole is draped over the back of the lawn chair, flapping in the breeze.

I have no idea what it means. Josie was better at dissecting dreams.

Next morning after the dream, there was a knock at my door. Maybe it was Josie, drunk, finally coming back home. I jumped out of bed, and peered through the ripped screen. It was the dealer. At first I backed away, but then it came to me: he'd killed Josie. Payback for the dog. And then there I was, slamming open my door, pouncing on the dealer, pinning him to the wall with my elbow. I held him for ten full seconds, breathing onto his ear, and then caught his eye. He smiled, then pushed me back into the mailbox, flashed a machete from the pocket of his hoodie and said, 'Where's my dog?'

When I saw the blade, my hands lifted in surrender and I slid down to my knees. I told him it was accident: I thought it was a coyote coming after my Josie. I begged him to tell me where Josie was and what he'd done to her. 'Stop fucking crying, man, stand the fuck up,' he said. 'I didn't touch your old woman. I'm here to talk business.' He demanded a pool in exchange for the dog. Deluxe. Worth thousands. Installed ASAP. Plus five hundred in cash. I had no choice but to accept the bargain.

After this, I glided into my lucid regrets. I wrote them down with a mind to release them: advice from the love-muscle experts.

I ignored bruises on my own mother's face, back when she was living out at the lake with Tinsel Tony.

I assumed my sister's heart surgery would be a breeze; that there was no need to call and wish her well.

I've never answered the phone on Christmas Day.

I couldn't burn the list and let the past go, like it said in the steps. I ended up crunching it into a ball and kicking it around the house.

A worry-free month is actually a suggestion I like, where you put off all your worries until the next month. I just don't have a month to try it. If Josie doesn't turn up in the next couple weeks to testify at the trial, the prosecutor said there won't be any hope of getting her ex convicted.

The dealer called a couple days ago, looking for his pool. There was still slush covering his grass, so he said to bring a shovel. I went over there and a woman came out. Brown teeth, skinny shaky arms. She pointed where she wanted the pool to go and went back inside. I'd been shovelling wet snow for an hour when I heard the creak of a door, the bark of a dog. The dealer came out with a Rottweiler pup at his feet. My nipples burned in pain at the sound of the dog: I longed for Josie. I focused on unpacking the parts of the pump, slipping them into my pocket. It was hard to breathe.

'Hey pool boy,' he called. 'Good news for ya. Saw your missus down the visitors' room at the ladies' prison.'

'Josie?' I said. 'Don't think so. She's left town.'

'Yea, Josie, that's her. Guard was calling her name. And I wouldn't forget those legs. She made a real show last week, couldn't keep her hands off her ladyfriend inside.'

His lip curled and he smiled. I looked down, punctured the plastic wrapping and ripped it out of the box. A sick, chemical smell wafted up at me. I clicked the in-valve into place, then the out-valve. I wrapped my hand around the round filter.

'Need you gone soon, pool boy,' he said. 'Somebody's coming by.'

I heard the door whine then snap closed behind him. I scraped the last of the snow, put the shovel down and picked up the pump. The moon rose up from behind the pines and I heard buzzing. It sounded like it was coming from inside the pump. I put it up to my ear and the hum grew louder, my eardrum began to vibrate. I opened the filter and tilted it into my palm.

There was nothing inside at all.

Hens' feet

JANE LAVELLE

1

Somewhere above the Arabian Gulf, Saira fell asleep. Minecraft and snacks had kept her going a long time, but the final thousand miles had been too much. I carried her through the airport, propping her head up for the immigration officials so they could see that she was the child pictured in her passport photo.

Amir was waiting for us at arrivals. I passed Saira into his arms, and he held her – and then me – in a reparatory embrace: we'd been apart for three months. Saira remained asleep while the car twisted among the Czech hedgehogs, meant to frustrate any vehicles set on storming the airport; nor did she open her eyes as we barrelled across the dark city to her grandmother's house. Between us, we untacked her body from the hot plastic seat, carried her into the house and laid her on the huge, low bed the three of us were to share.

Amir's mother was still up. She had sweet tea boiling on the hob and carried two cups up the stairs, handing mine over with a salty kiss. She sat on the edge of the bed, resting her hands close to the child's bare legs, not touching for fear of waking her.

Amir had come to Karachi to shepherd his mother through an operation and the long convalescence it required. Even now, Ammi-ji was not quite in possession of her full physical strength, although her wits were unaffected. The plan was to stay a few weeks, then bring her back with us to Belfast, where she could complete her recovery in the care of her only son.

Ammi-ji watched her granddaughter for a long time, without speaking, as

I drank the tea and Amir dug pyjamas and toothbrushes out of our bags for us. When she finally spoke again it was to him, softly and in Urdu.

'She looks just like you.'

According to family folklore, Amir was a child so beautiful he couldn't move for offers of marriage. On the day he was born, two hospital doctors attempted to claim his hand on behalf of their daughters, yet unborn.

2

The last time I had been in Karachi, nine years previously, was for a wedding – my own and Amir's.* Our daughter was with us then, too, an early thickening of the belly. At that time, the atmosphere in the city had been hard to parse. There was, I thought, a feeling of looming disaster mixed in with the everyday tumult. But I was a stranger, newly pregnant and sensitive to risk. I couldn't tell how much of this I was imagining.

Looking back, though, it wasn't just me. A few weeks after we left, the Taliban descended on Karachi Airport with grenades in their pockets and rocket launchers on their backs. They wrote off two full-size aircraft; many people died. Between sectarian violence, assassinations and terrorist attacks, three thousand Karachiites were killed that year.

Now, the city seemed different. It felt cleaner; I thought the roads were less ragged. There were still guns around – and they were just as huge and casually handled as before – but there seemed to be fewer of them, and they were mostly in the hands of people wearing uniforms. Once, when we stopped at a petrol station, I watched a young cashier flick for change through a wad of notes as thick as his wrist. He must have been glad of his guard.

But Amir warned me against conclusions drawn from early impressions. Some things were better, yes, but others were much worse. There were new

*See 'Wedding Pictures', Dublin Review 69 (Winter 2017–18).

privations, caused by inflation and the effects of the pandemic. Fuel was all but unaffordable now and flour was in short supply. A rumour was circulating that tea itself was becoming scarce. Amir had created a small stockpile in the basement, next to the emergency generator.

As for improvements in the infrastructure, some of those were shallow, others illusory. Take the manhole covers. Imran Khan's government had replaced these across the entire city but, instead of using cast iron for the frames, they had gone for some cheap composite. The material couldn't withstand the city's relentless, and rising, heat levels. The frames had begun to melt and the metal lids to drop into the sewers, leaving hot black gaps in the roads.

Amir began to point out uncovered manholes. After he'd shown me a couple, I noticed them everywhere. How did people avoid them, I asked, in the traffic, when they couldn't see past the riksha in front?

He shrugged. 'You live here for a while, there are things you get to know.'

We had the use of a boxy hatchback, of a sort ubiquitous in all but the swankiest neighbourhoods of the city. It belonged to a cousin of Amir's, who was content to make do with his motorcycle for as long as we were here. As we zipped around the city, Saira sat in the back with me; Amir took the passenger seat. A local man, Manaver, did the driving.

Until recently, Manaver had been a lift attendant in the offices of *Dawn*, an English-language newspaper. That job had disappeared, but Manaver still had options. When Amir's father built his house thirty years ago, the surrounding area was populated by villagers from rural Sindh, who were loosely organized into workers' groups with political affiliations. Those groups still existed and, come election time, delivered votes by various means. But they had long ago abandoned activism. Instead, they hijacked cars and fenced the parts, ran protection, dealt drugs. They used the area's poor as foot soldiers, putting them to dirty and dangerous work.

A man of Manaver's capabilities, though, could be more than just cannon fodder. It would be easy for him to throw in his lot with the gangs, to work a little and be paid a lot. But so far he had resisted, instead doing odd jobs for local matriarchs and getting by on whatever they managed to pay him. He was a good friend of Amir's, the two having grown up together, and generally respected for his moral fibre.

Manaver came with us whenever we left the house. He was part companion, part bodyguard. With me he was all but silent, maintaining a scrupulous physical distance. Once or twice I tried to force eye contact, to thank him for opening the car door or helping Saira across a road. But, short of turning his face with my hand, I couldn't make him look at me. This was annoying, although I knew better than to mistake it for coldness.

Saira had more luck. She chatted incessantly in Manaver's direction and with her he was softer. On one occasion he even smiled, revealing, in a face of austerely regular features, a pair of goofy, crooked front teeth.

3

The Saturday of our first weekend was a religious feast, and there was a party in another house in the family compound. It was an annual occasion, but this year more guests than usual were expected, because Amir and his wife and child had returned from Europe. Naturally, people would want a look at us.

The house had belonged to Amir's great-uncle, who'd lived there with his three wives and umpteen children until his death. Now he presided over the place from a photo above the living-room door, his hair and moustache neat and slick, his gaze lordly. Only the last of the unmarried sons lived in the house now, although the daughters came back in a din of pots and pans for occasions like this one. Rabia, not the eldest of the sisters but certainly the loudest, was in charge.

The party began at dusk. Chairs were distributed in the courtyard outside, beneath the Shia standard and the great coconut tree on which fruits were already ripening. When we arrived, a game of ice and water – a kind of freeze-tag – was already going on among the children. Saira kept one eye on it, absorbing the rules even as she and I were presented in turn to a score of admiring relations. As soon as she could, she slipped away and melted into the game.

I sat down beside Hamza, who was Rabia's husband and the youngest of Amir's many uncles. Rabia and Hamza were first cousins. Cousin marriage was accepted here – preferred, in fact, sometimes, especially where there was property to consolidate. Throughout Amir's childhood, it had been loosely understood that one of his mother's nieces was intended for him. If he had stayed in Pakistan, he told me, he would likely have married her. She had not come to the party.

Hamza offered me a glass of sugar-cane juice. It looked like puddle water and smelled like grass, so the moment of cold, nectarous rapture the first sip delivered took me by surprise.

'Good, no?'

I nodded and drank again.

Hamza was a big man. He had tight white stubble with crisp edges and wrinkles under his eyes. He spoke in confident but inexact English, catching hold of his clever eldest son now and again and asking him to translate the odd tricky concept. It was religion he was talking about, mostly. The mullahs and maulanas were getting it all wrong.

'The only thing we need is the Holy Qur'an,' he said, 'and it's not hard to interpret.'

'OK,' I said.

'Women are required to dress modestly, but then so are men. There is no need to wear hijab. No need to stay at home.' I looked around for Rabia, who had worked as a flight attendant before she was married. I couldn't see her, but her voice was coming from the kitchen.

'I love Nelson Mandela,' said Hamza. 'And Mother Teresa, she's my favourite.'

I watched a rout of mosquitoes forming above his head. One of the bites I was already carrying, on my upper thigh, had brought up a lump so big it was visible through my loose-fitting *salwar*. Anyone who grew up here would be partially immune to the dengue and malaria rising from the river, but Saira and I were on the back foot.

'I'm reading the Bhagavad Gita,' Hamza went on. 'Have you read it?'

I confessed I hadn't. There was no alcohol at the party and I couldn't detect any smell, but Hamza had a woolly look in his eyes and I wondered about it. The mosquitoes were around my ears now, making a low, human sort of hum. I was glad when Rabia called us in for dinner.

The women had prepared food in clay pots, as was customary for this particular feast, and spread it out on the living-room floor. There was chicken biryani and mutton curry, with yoghurty lentil fritters and rice pudding flavoured with cardamom. I piled food onto my plate and began to eat. I wasn't used to sitting on the floor, though, and soon retreated to the sofa on a pair of dead legs.

A tall man with a luxuriant black quiff arrived and gave a *salaam* to the company, apologizing cheerfully for his lateness. This was Mohammed Ali, one of Rabia's brothers. Mohammed Ali had been at our wedding, but I didn't remember him. He was, anyhow, a changed man, having recently had a hair transplant. Before he sat down he did a lap of the room, allowing the older aunties to touch the gelled thatch at his forehead. They remarked on its plenitude and wished him health to wear it.

Rabia handed Mohammed Ali a plate. I examined his hair as he ate, trying to tell the old stuff from the new. I couldn't – it was an excellent job. He noticed me looking and laughed, then produced on his phone pictures of his former, much balder head.

Mohammed Ali worked in *Dawn*'s finance department. He had excellent English and an interest in books. I was planning to attend a literary festival in a few days' time, I told him. He had wanted to go too, but couldn't get the time off work. We talked about a Turkish writer we both admired and he bemoaned the fact that Amazon didn't yet operate in Pakistan.

'It's not that we can't get foreign books,' he said, 'but they're pirated copies. Poor-quality paper, smudged ink. They're very difficult to read.' I took his address and a wish list, promising to send parcels in the post.

Bilal, an uncle on Ammi-ji's side, had come equipped with old photo albums and was passing them around. The photos were mostly of himself and his nine siblings, including Ammi-ji, in whose features I could trace the same trenchant composure over sixty-odd years. There were no photos of their parents, who had come to Karachi in the great migration that followed Partition in 1947. Thinking that Saira ought to know her own history, I once asked Amir what he knew about that time. Not much, he said, except that it was horrific beyond words. It was not discussed, as a rule. People knew better than to bring it up.

Next came a small set of six-by-four prints, reverently presented by Bilal, depicting Imran Khan: in his cricketing days; at home, posed in virile relaxation, the wall behind him patterned with tigers; with his then-wife Jemima, Princess Diana and a Pakistani bodyguard, out and about in Karachi or Islamabad.

'That was a difficult breakup for us, Imran and Jemima,' Bilal told me. 'Our hearts are still broken about it.'

Hamza had been disappearing every so often into the empty portions of the house and making increasingly dramatic re-entrances. He sashayed across the room now, to whoops of appreciation from Rabia and the younger women. Bilal got up and made space for him; Ammi-ji folded her arms and crossed her legs.

The talk had turned to drugs. Lately there had been nightly gatherings in some of the gullies around the compound. There were the seasoned addicts, looking for heroin, which still streamed across the border from Afghanistan and was sold, mixed with other, unknown substances, in blocks the size and shape of a hotel soap-cake. Into these, users would stick a metal skewer, heated to redness, and inhale the vertical plume of smoke through a straw. New to the area, and gaining a foothold, was crystal meth. No one knew much about it yet but everyone was worried by the wilder brand of user now at large on the streets. The periodic sackings of the area by the army, who rooted the old out of their beds and hauled off the young en masse, were not looked forward to by anyone. All the same, the company agreed, it was high time one took place.

Hamza produced some sachets from his pocket, tossing them to a few of the men.

'Pakistani cocaine,' he said to me, emptying one into his mouth. I knew about *gutka*. It was a mixture of betel nut and tobacco. It was addictive and gave you mouth cancer – Amir knew people who had died because of it. It was illegal, he had told me, but not exactly difficult to find.

Hamza leaned over.

'We are good people in Pakistan,' he said, 'but our leaders are corrupt. Each one as bad as the next.'

'What about Imran Khan?' I asked. I looked for Bilal. He was in a corner with Amir, talking him through one of the albums.

'Oh!' said Hamza. 'Very bad guy. Involved with women ... men ... everything. Bad character.'

Saira had come in from the yard. It was dark now and she had tripped on a loose tile, cutting her knee. Amir scooped her up as she crossed the room and set her on his lap. He hummed an Urdu song in her ear.

Hamza made a sideways chopping motion with his hand. 'Corrupt.' He had his head tilted back now and his lower jaw was jutting. Betel juice, red like blood, gathered beneath his tongue.

Ammi-ji had kept a stack of *salwar kameezen* for me, tucked away in a wardrobe, from the time of the wedding. These were what most Pakistani women wore from day to day – light, loose trousers with a long tunic over the top. They flattered at the waist, forgave at the rear and came with a *dupatta*, a long scarf that could be configured in exciting ways. I loved *salwar kameezen* and looked forward to wearing them. Tonight I had picked out a gold tunic embroidered in red. My *dupatta* was made of some smooth, diaphanous fabric, which I had opened out over my shoulders and bunched around my wrists. I felt lavish and contented, a strawberry creme in a shiny wrapper.

'You look lovely,' said Rabia, arranging the *dupatta* into a better-favoured shape. 'A good choice for a dinner party.' She paused. 'This book festival, though …'

'A book show, sure,' interjected Ammi-ji, 'but it'll be a fashion show too.'

'Oh, believe me,' said Rabia.

My outfits for the festival had already been the subject of discussion at home. Apparently they would take some planning.

'*He* thinks a Balochi dress,' said Ammi-ji, pointing at Amir.

'Oh no,' said Rabia.

'Very much in fashion,' ventured a pale woman in a budgie-yellow dress, whose name was Zainab.

'But you have to know how to wear them,' said Ammi-ji.

'Exactly. Don't forget,' Rabia said, circling her face with her finger, 'she's already going to stand out. What about a *kurta* and a pair of jeans?'

'I think a *salwar kameez*,' said Ammi-ji. 'Well cut, with a tasteful print.'

'Well,' said Rabia. 'Just don't put her in one of those puffy things. She'll look like she's just off the plane.'

The women laughed. I did too, but said nothing. Zainab eyed me curiously, then spoke to Amir.

'She hasn't changed since the wedding, your wife,' said Zainab. 'A quiet woman.'

Amir smiled. 'Don't worry. She'll be paying attention.'

'Indeed she will,' said Rabia, 'this writer.' They looked at me and, for the first time in a long time, there was a small hush. The atmosphere tightened.

'Main soon rahi hoon,' I said. *I'm listening.*

5

There was no connecting door between the coconut-tree house and Amir's, so we had to leave the compound to make the short walk home. The night air would be almost sweet on Amir's rooftop, but down here in the gully it was suffocating. Food smells mixed with animal dung and fumes from the main road. The power, subject to a rolling schedule of outages, was not due back on for another hour and the streets, though still busy, were black as ink. In the darkness, funnelled between high walls, every sound – every shuffling footstep – seemed dramatically close. I held Saira's hand; she held Ammi-ji's. We followed Amir around one corner and then another. Something I couldn't see emitted a blat at my elbow. I deduced a goat, but I couldn't be sure.

In the street we came to now, a motorcycle headlamp shone out of a recess, casting a shaft across to the opposite side. I could see the figure of a man blocking our way. He looked like he was holding something.

We stopped. Amir spoke to the man quietly, in words I didn't understand and a tone I couldn't interpret. He spoke back.

Amir turned. 'Come here,' he said to Saira, drawing her forward by the shoulder. Then he spoke to me. 'Give me your phone.'

I handed it over. He found the torch, turned it on and directed it at the man's hands. In his palm, compact and elegant, was a turtle. Its head was stretched forward but its eyes were closed and it was swaying. The shell was painted and varnished, each segment a different colour. The man turned the turtle over and ran his knuckles along its waxen belly.

'It's a baby,' he said, holding it out towards Saira.

Saira took it. She carried it ahead of her as we walked, the man at our side, the rest of the way home. He came with us as far as Ammi-ji's front door, where we gave the animal back.

A couple of days later, Manaver drove us to the zoo. It was early when we got there and the place was almost deserted. Around the entrance were peacocks and flamingos. We made our way among them for a while, then watched a pair of crocodiles heave and disappear into their pickle-coloured pond. An old man with a forked metal stick approached to entice us into the reptile house.

'Little snakes?' he said to Saira in English. Saira took my hand.

The reptile house was a one-roomed building, with big glass cases all around the walls. Each case contained a different species and the man was entering them, one by one, through a hatch in the back. He was applying his rod to the least lively of the snakes, prodding them off their rocks and branches. If that wasn't enough to rouse them, he used his hands. It worked: they hissed, contorted, put on a show.

One of the cases contained a pair of Indian rock pythons. The old man lifted the first with both hands and threw it on top of its fellow, which set them writhing together along the length of the glass. My throat constricted and I wanted to get out, but Saira, gripping my fingers to numbness now, was grimly captivated. To our relief, the old man didn't penetrate the last enclosure, in which glossy black cobras were alert and swaying.

He escorted us to the 'animal museum', another large, square building. There we had to buy special tickets for entry. The sign on the door advertised taxidermic displays for zoological research. The creatures inside were rattily stuffed and arranged in tableaux of nightmarish oddity. There was a markhor – a large goat, the national animal of Pakistan – aiming its corkscrew horns at a mountain lion, which already carried in its mouth a fawn, slumped in a bloody parabola. The teeth and claws of all the animals were brokenly authentic, but the eyes were plastic and, judging by their brightness and perfection, recently installed in a job lot. They were amber-coloured and far too big, giving each creature a look of exaggerated terror. The mongoose, with its huge, mad, orange eyes, was particularly horrifying. Saira was pale and silent now, holding her father's hand as well as mine.

Near the exit was a notice proclaiming a very special exhibit – the world's only four-legged chicken. The creature in question was tiny, but better stuffed than some of its more exotic stablemates. It had, at least, its own eyes. The area around its thighs had been doctored with white feathers, manifestly plastic, and from among these protruded a second pair of real hen's legs and feet. Its beak was open in what looked like horrified dismay, as if it had just realized what they'd done to it.

I was confused. Was this some kind of joke? The giraffes and zebras outside were real and we hadn't needed special tickets to see them. Why would anyone pay money for this?

'Look around,' said Amir. 'It's not the exhibits we've paid for. It's the air con.' Sure enough, almost everyone in the building was gathered around the big electric fans in the corners. We were the only idiots looking at the chicken.

Back outside, Amir and Manaver went to buy some fizzy orange from a vendor with a refrigerated handcart. Saira and I waited in the shade of a fat-trunked date palm. The snake-hassler was loitering in the background with his stick, keeping half an eye on us. I hoped he wasn't planning on poking a tiger.

Some chattering girls passed, dressed handsomely in sequins and lipstick. The sight of us gave rise to whispers and curious looks, but we were getting used to this by now. The girls slowed, turned and came back with a request: could they take a few selfies? They posed with us as if we were family, resting their elbows on our shoulders and kissing our cheeks. After they had thanked us and moved on, another group stepped forward.

'You speak Urdu?' one of the young women asked.

'A little,' I said, then fielded some genial questions about where we came from and what we were doing here. By the time Amir came back there was a queue forming, but they seemed to lose confidence when he joined us and handed over the drinks. He was laughing.

'Let's move,' he said, 'before they glue an extra pair of feet on you.'

Amir disappeared into a dark building that might have been an office, emerging a few minutes later with a man in uniform, who had a pistol on his belt and a set of keys in his hand. He led us towards a massive gate up ahead.

'The Mughal Garden is closed to the public,' the man said in English, 'but you have come a long way. So on this occasion we are pleased to admit you.'

As the man unlocked the gate, I wondered whether money had changed hands in the dark. When he left us, locking us in, he said, 'But – we request that you take plenty of photos. Social media.'

The garden was magnificent. It was laid out in perfect symmetry, with mosaic paths bordered by flowerbeds and a pavilion at one end, delicately ornamented with holed stone screens. We walked up one side of the central water channel and down the other. Beyond the spiked border railings was a platform from which visitors could view the garden. A small crowd gathered there now, but it was us rather than the flowers they were looking at.

Amir dipped the edge of his sandal into the water, causing a small ripple.

'When I was a kid, this garden was open to everyone,' he said, 'but they trashed the place.'

A small distance ahead, Saira was whacking something in the water with a stick: a dead black kite. It seemed to me that she was taking out on the animal some of the stress caused by thrashing reptiles and taxidermy she couldn't unsee. I thought of a passage from Nabokov:

> If churches speak to us of the Gospel, zoos remind us of the solemn, and tender, beginning of the Old Testament. The only sad part is that this artificial Eden is all behind bars, although it is also true that if there were no enclosures the very first dingo would savage me.

6

On the evening before we left, we went to say goodbye to the neighbours. The doors from the street were all open – it seemed that Ammi-ji was the only one who locked hers – and Amir breezed in and out of them with childhood familiarity. The doors gave onto courtyards, which led in turn to dark rooms crammed with belongings.

Most of the people we called on had been at Rabia's party, among a second wave of guests who arrived and ate after the family had finished. All of them stood up when we arrived and greeted us graciously. The women raised their *dupatten* over their heads. I found myself doing the same, although I had felt no pressure or desire to do this until now – even at the vast marble tomb of Mohammed Ali Jinnah, where the women wore the *burqa* and shoes were not allowed.

One of the places we came to was the room Manaver shared with his wife, Nusrat, and their one-year-old son. It was part of a building inhabited by several families. Everyone so far had offered us something to eat or drink, but Amir had said no – we had a lot of visits to get through. Here, though, we stopped. Manaver held the baby while Nusrat made some tea. For want of space inside, we drank standing in a patch of sun in the centre of the courtyard. A sober-faced, sand-coloured cow watched us from the corner, blinking away flies.

The arrangements for Manaver's marriage had been fraught, Amir had told me. Nusrat's people were not wealthy, but she was educated; Manaver, for all his aptitudes, could not read or write. Talks between the two families had been close to breaking down at one point. It was Ammi-ji who had stepped in to close the deal.

Nusrat and Manaver seemed well suited: they had the same impassive dignity. As usual, Manaver was avoiding eye-contact, but Nusrat was looking at me directly, with an expression I could not read. I tried to work out what she was thinking, but doing so made me feel exposed. I was aware of the barbarous tack of my silver sandals, and of my feet inside them, white and puffed up in the heat like deployed airbags. Standing there in my embroidered *kameez* and glittery *dupatta*, in the full glare of the sun, I felt as foppish as a macaw. I was in danger of burning, so I stepped back into the shade.

When we got home, Ammi-ji was covering her three-piece suite with sheets in preparation for her lengthy absence. 'The house is going to be empty,' she said. 'There'll be dust an inch deep when I get back. What did you think of these locals?' I noticed she didn't use the word *paroseeon*, 'neighbours'. 'Simple people, no?'

7

Back in Belfast, unpacking her bags, Saira came across an envelope Nusrat had handed her as we left. It contained a thousand-rupee note. She brought it in to school to show her classmates. The teacher went online. The man pictured on the note, according to Wikipedia, was a prominent barrister and politician who had been instrumental in the foundation of Pakistan. The banknote was worth about three pounds sterling, the teacher said, the price of a cup of coffee.

Saira brought the note home again, annoyed at her teacher's lack of vision. She preferred to reckon its value in other ways: in varnished turtles, perhaps, or adventures by riksha. She returned it to its envelope and has left it in the keeping-box under her bed. She will need it, she says, whenever she goes back.

... must be destroyed ...

RICHARD LEA

He stands there in front of the low glass cabinet staring at the pale pile of catapult stones, the lozenge phalanx of lead sling bullets, the blackened javelin tip. He stands there as the babble from the tour guide in the corner washes over him, as the teenager's smartphone swooshes an image of a two-thousand-year-old leather sack up into the cloud. He stands there in the museum's clear, white light with his relaxed-fit cargo shorts and his lo-rise Converse and all he sees is darkness.

At breakfast a sea breeze was ghosting up off the beach across the rooftop terrace, the first breath of autumn after four days of flat heat. Sarah had slept through the muezzin's crackling wail, so he'd scooped up the baby, changed her nappy, crept out of the room. It had been a long night.

They followed a waitress to a table by the pool and stood while she set up a high chair. He plopped Kate in it, velcroed her crinkly book to the tray and handed her Rabbit. She grabbed it tight to her chest and gazed out over the bay, legs paddling steadily as she chewed on its ear. He turned on his phone. Da, da, ba da, ba gah. Down on the waterfront, palm trees stirred and waves curtained the strip of sand. A cargo ship perched almost at the horizon, insubstantial with distance. A ferry carved in towards the port.

Ping and rattle from the phone on the glass tabletop. He flipped it over. Anya: *Did you tell her yet?*

A couple of taps to delete the message, then the phone in his pocket and around the other side to scoop up Kate and go check out the breakfast buffet. Baguette, melon, ham. A basket of pastries and a selection of prepared fruits. Chilled butter. A platter of dates. Insurgents advancing across the cover of the complimentary *New York Times*. Ba, da, ba, gah dah. Warm in the crook of his arm. He served himself a bowl of granola one-handed, topped it with red berries and a spoon of yoghurt. Why was Anya stressing? It must have been past midnight back in San Francisco.

Sarah was still dozing when they got back to the room. She reached for the bedside lamp as he pulled the door shut behind him, then sat up in bed with her glasses on to eat the roll and coffee he'd brought. He drew back the curtains, stretched out a blanket for Kate by the window, surrounded her with pillows and handed her the jangly ball. He batted it back to her a few times – clever girl – handed her a couple of plastic cups, sat down in one of the armchairs and looked out over the old town towards the chunky minaret by the market.

　　– Maybe we should get going, Prof. Before the heat.

　　– Uh huh.

　　– Otherwise we won't make it to your museum.

Sarah swigged the last of the coffee, sighed and stumbled to the bathroom, wrapping herself in a towel. The skoosh and thrum of the shower. A Walmart wreathed in fire and tear gas on CNN. Kate gumming at the rim of a purple cup. Unh, unh, erh. He checked his phone. Nothing. A sigh. A yawn. He reached out to the bedside table behind him for Sarah's book.

As the crackling flames appear on high, Aeneas clothes his shoulders with a lion's hide, loads his father on his bending back and turns his feet towards a ruined temple without the city walls – his son tripping along with unequal paces beside him, his wife following after. Seized with fear at every shadow, he strays through every dark and every devious way while Troy burns around him.

> Till, near the ruin'd gate arriv'd at last,
> Secure, and deeming all the danger past,

A frightful noise of trampling feet we hear.

My father, looking thro' the shades, with fear,

Cried out: 'Haste, haste, my son, the foes are nigh;

Their swords and shining armor I descry.'

Some hostile god, for some unknown offense,

Had sure bereft my mind of better sense;

For, while thro' winding ways I took my flight,

And sought the shelter of the gloomy night,

Alas! I lost Creusa …

By the time they got out of the hotel, the sun was looming above the palm trees, bludgeoning the road with heat. The taxi man bowed and nodded as he opened the boot for the buggy, rucksack and changing bag. Sarah pulled at her seatbelt, tugging it around Kate in the BabyBjörn.

— Did you do the sun cream?

— Yes.

— What about the back of her legs?

— Yes.

— Monsieur, monsieur. Sidi Bou Said, monsieur?

Greying stubble, yellowing teeth. A wet cough. Sarah leaned away, winding down the window.

— Oui monsieur. Sidi Bou Said. Au pied de la colline, s'il vous plaît.

Turning back.

— Did you put in another hat?

— Yes. And a change of clothes. And two bottles of milk.

The air was cooler when they were out of the taxi, in the shade of the winding alleys. Kate bumped and joggled up the narrow pavements in the buggy, Sarah muttering about the uneven cobbles.

They stopped for lunch at a café overlooking a small square near the top of the hill. Kate drank a bottle in the buggy as they waited for their mak-loubs. She didn't seem to want any sleep, fussing and kicking, batting the proffered toys straight down on to the dirty paving, so he hauled her out – one, two, three – and bounced her on his knee while he ate. A ping from his phone and he put down his fork, switched Kate over to the other leg and fished it out. Anya again. Delete.

– Who is it?

– Just work stuff.

– I thought we said no phones.

– Sorry. Was just checking the disease advisory earlier.

– What's the latest?

– Just the same seven countries. They're not even bothering to test people who've changed planes in Africa yet, even if it's sub-Saharan.

He locked the phone and put it back into his pocket, Kate squirming and reaching for his fries. He moved the plate to the side and pushed back his glass, leaving a teaspoon for her to chew on in the middle of the space he'd cleared. She grabbed it and started banging it on the iron table instead, riding his swaying knee with cowboy ease, grinning at the resounding clang. Ah! Ahwah!

A wide smile from the young man in mirror shades at the next table.

– He is very strong baby.

Sarah put her knife and fork back on the plate and signalled to the waiter.

– You can put her in now. We're going.

The little yellow cab they hailed at the bottom of the hill had a big dent in the front wing and deep gouges along the doors. The driver gestured with his thumb when Sarah asked if they could put the buggy in the boot, then turned and yelled to be careful when they slammed it shut. The seatbelt on her side was jammed. They switched places. The taxi man nodded when Sarah asked him to take them to the museum, but ten minutes later, after barrelling past a couple of clearly marked turns at breakneck speed, he slowed to a crawl with the meter still whirling and started craning his head to left and right. An awkward exchange with Sarah, a hair-raising swerve across the highway and he deposited them in the blunt heat at the bottom of a flight of steps. A plastic bag hung in the dry tangle of thorns and bushes by the side of the deserted road, bottles and cans strewn along the kerb. The museum was at the top, he said. There was no question of going further on to look for another entrance.

As soon as they got through the museum gates they unfolded the buggy, reclining the seat in the hope Kate might fall asleep as they wheeled her over the level crown of the hill. Er, er. Ahberh. Sarah stowed the BabyBjörn in the webbing underneath, dabbed with a wet wipe at the mark the seatbelt had left on her white T-shirt and strode off towards an information panel. He trundled behind, picking his way past a line of cypresses. Hunks of damaged statuary on pedestals between each one.

He stopped at the edge of the esplanade, looking out across fields and ruined arches to the port and the bay below. An airliner nosing its way through the haze, winking in the heavy sun. Bah, er. Ba-dah. Patchy grass between piles of rubble.

— They flattened the whole city after the siege. Built another one right on top of it.

Sarah sweeping her arm in lecture mode.

— The houses over there were preserved under a huge layer of rubble. Let's take a look.

He told her he wouldn't bother going down the narrow stairs – said the ground on the lower level was too uneven for the buggy anyhow. He'd wait up here with Kate, see if he could get her to sleep. Sarah clumped down the steps, shaking her head, while he curved the buggy towards a patch of shade by the main building. Kate's babble rose up into an almost cry, then subsided as she finally drifted off, a tiny fist wrapped tight round Rabbit's ear. Another ping from his phone: *You better tell her before you get back.* Delete.

The gift shop and café were both closed. He pushed the buggy up along-side a low bench under the cedars and sat there scuffing at the gravel with his sneakers until Sarah spotted them.

— Has she been out long?

— Little while.

A coachload of old people ambled past the bench and through the arch into the courtyard, the mustachioed guide barking at them in Italian — or was it Spanish?

— I'll sit with her a bit. It's nice in the shade. You go in.

He followed the group into the gallery, past mosaics and pottery, lamps and pale brown plates. They gathered around a set of statues at the far end while the guide launched into his spiel, shifting on their sandals, fanning themselves with leaflets as they craned to peer at the mute sarcophagi.

A blank look from the giant head at the turn of the stairs and the clear light of the second floor washed over him, the tour party shuffling up the steps behind. They bumbled past him towards a case in the corner with a dis-play showing amphoras of differing design, but he came to a halt beside a low glass cabinet.

THE SIEGE — 146BC

Byrsa hill was destroyed and burned along with the rest of the city, with the Punic quarter buried under a layer of rubble two meters thick.

'We noticed a change in the colour of the earth, which gradually became blacker as we continued to dig. Standing walls began to appear, as well as a large quantity of shards mixed with ash, car-bonized detritus and pieces of burned wood.'

— Jean Ferron and Maurice Pinard 1955

The javelin tip (5) was discovered by the remains of a wounded soldier.

'When Scipio thought that a sufficient number of troops had entered the town, he gave leave to the larger number of them to attack those in it, according to the Roman custom, with directions to kill everything they met, and to spare nothing; and not to begin looting until they got the order to do so. The object of this is, I suppose, to strike terror. Accordingly, one may often see in towns captured by the Romans, not only human beings who have been put to the sword, but even dogs cloven down the middle, and the limbs of other animals hewn off. On this occasion the amount of such slaughter was exceedingly great, because of the numbers included in the city.'

— Polybius Histories 10.15

He stands there in front of the cabinet and stares. A small pile of pale, round stones. A squadron of diamond-shaped pellets. A blade, bent and blackened.

And death rises up about him in bright orange hazmat suits,

in turbans and dirty sweatpants,

wrapped in the Confederate flag.

It tumbles off the back of dusty pickups waving AK-47s and rocket-propelled grenades,

it surges down the pavement brandishing flick knives and baseball bats.

Here it comes rolling off the ocean like an express train twenty storeys high,

here it is streaking through the atmosphere like a flaming mountain, an avenging star.

It is cold, inevitable, slow.

There's no power and the phones are down and the storm outside the window is yowling like a hungry child. He grabs a pack of nappies and some formula and a bottle and a change of clothes and stuffs them in a rucksack, wraps Kate in another blanket and heads out into the hall. The flashlight splays shadows down the stairwell out in front of him, the blackness follows on behind. But when he gets to the basement it's five feet deep in churning water, cars sloshing into each other in the gloom like grinning bergs. Out through the ruined gate into the brute wind with the rain battering his shoulders, spattering his hood as he hunches over the child. He stumbles on for a block or two through darkened streets, winding left and right past shattered windows and burned-out shops. The mangled corpse of a scrawny cat. Torches in the distance – a gang coming towards him on the other side of the street. He ducks into a doorway, shrinks back into the corner as they lope by. He stands there under the shelter of the tattered awning with the sour tang of ash at the back of his throat, with Kate warm in his arms. And he has lost Sarah.

My father's things

JOE DAVIES

1

My father died in hospital in Parry Sound, Ontario, on the 3rd of September 2016. He was ninety-two, a fairly reputable age for someone who'd spent a good deal of his life sitting on his ass, smoking a pipe, painting, disarming people with his boyish charm and dazzling them with his chiselled ideas about what looked good. He was a man who knew how to get what he wanted. And when it suited him he knew how to retreat into a sort of child-like helplessness. I saw it often enough to know what I was looking at. When dementia crept in and the veneer fell away, what was left was the boy – the naughty boy – wanting it all his own way. And I hate to think just how much I'm like him.

As a child, I didn't blame him for my parents' divorce. But by my mid-twenties I saw how lightly and easily he'd managed to sidestep the bulk of my growing up. What I saw was a successful man – a *very* successful man – who pampered himself, while I grew up in the strange mess of a rooming house my mother kept to make ends meet.

I often wondered what he thought of himself, or if he ever gave himself a solid look. I remember once asking him one of the harder questions. We were on the train back to Toronto after visiting his sister in Belleville – I would have been in my early twenties – and I asked what he would have done for a living if he hadn't wound up with the talent he had, the talent his career as a commercial illustrator stood on. It was a prodding sort of question, one I unreasonably hoped would lead him to admit how lucky *he* was, but also help him to intuit how at sea *I* felt just then. Bike courier, kitchen drudge, even university student – all I wished for in these phases was an escape hatch.

But he was unable to be the father I needed in that moment, one who could imagine what it was like to be me, and who could see that I was stuck. He either couldn't or wouldn't see it, and instead became almost gruff in response to my question – gruff in a way I never really saw in him before that, or after – suggesting I'd hit a nerve of some kind. He said, 'I'd have thought of something.' No doubt he would have. Really, I was asking the wrong person, someone who liked to keep to the shallows. Part of it, I suppose, was that he'd tasted enough disappointment in his fatherless, poverty-stricken youth and had simply decided to give any suggestion of despair a wide berth whenever it flickered, a berth so wide he could comfortably pretend there was no such thing. As my mother used to say of him, 'He was good at the fun stuff,' meaning he pretty much dodged the rest – the heartache, the mundane, compassion, just being there.

2

He could be very observant – of certain things, anyway. I have two memories of occasions when he commented on people seated at tables near us. In the first he leans across the table as if to share some secret and then proceeds to speak in a very loud voice, saying, 'The man at the table next to us is wearing a toupée.' In the second it's much the same, only this time when he leans forward it's to say, 'The woman at the next table is not a woman.' These were the kinds of things that caught his attention – these and beautiful women, beautiful in ways you'd probably expect.

Of course, he had to put up with me as well. I remember once we were out at his favourite lunch spot, the Coffee Mill, and he pointed out that Frank Mahovlich, the famous hockey player, was at the cash register paying up. For me, in my juvenile hockey-card-collecting madness, hearing this was like being jolted with a cattle prod. I was unable to think of anything but running directly for Mr Mahovlich. And as I stood, it sent almost everything on our table clattering to the floor, a noise that only served to detract from what was meant to be an otherwise perfect moment of fan–superstar interaction. I ran out the door after Mahovlich, but it was like one of those tricks in movies. Every time I followed him round a corner it was to find he was even farther away than before, until he was simply a dot in the distance, my vague notion of whatever it was I was hoping to obtain shrinking along with the sight of him.

When I returned to the Coffee Mill, they were very kind, and had replaced the orange sherbet I'd sent to the floor – at least, that's how I want to remember it. Orange sherbet, Wiener schnitzel, these were what I always ate when I went to The Coffee Mill with my father, and I'm sure it hasn't come across yet, but when I was young I was so proud of him – so proud that later in life it was a strange, off-balancing turnaround to discover I no longer felt that way.

It came in stages, I suppose, seeing him for who he was. One moment in particular might have begun the shift that would pull him into some sort of focus, though I expect I wouldn't have quite seen it at the time. We were down in Prince Edward County, close to where he grew up. I'd have been somewhere in my mid-teens. We'd come in his Jaguar, a car that was as unreliable as it was eye-catching. For a car that'd been built for a maritime country known for being a little on the rainy side, it was remarkably difficult to start whenever things got damp, which was what happened. So we had to find things to do close to where we were staying. He'd brought along an air pistol – he often seemed to have one of these – but finding somewhere we could use it proved a bit of a challenge. We wandered down the nearest road for a while, a road with cottages on one side and farmland on the other. Eventually my father spied what he was looking for, a raised bank of dirt running along one side of an empty field. It seemed a bit exposed and I'm pretty sure I said as much, but my father pressed on, saying it'd be fine. We walked in from the road, fifty yards or so, and set up a few bits and pieces in the bank of dirt, things to aim at – sticks, bottle caps, that sort of thing.

We took turns. First me, then him. I'm not sure how else to describe it: there was always something about target practice with an air pistol that got boring fairly quickly. We weren't at it long, though, before someone was striding across the dirt towards us. When my father understood what was about to happen he turned to me and said, 'I'll show you how to handle this.' And he did.

When the man drew close he said, 'You can't do that here' – his land, apparently – adding, 'It's not OK,' gesturing at the pistol.

On hearing this, my father manifested something close to surprise, then opened the taps of apology, saying, 'Oh, I didn't realize' and 'We're sorry' and a couple of other things to that effect. A credible performance – or, credible enough. What did I learn from it? First, that one workable strategy for navigating life includes appearing oblivious and becoming fawningly contrite whenever useful. Second, that my father was something of a sneak.

3

For a long while the reasons for my parents' divorce were a mystery to me. In some ways they still are. On one of my last visits to my father in his own home – before the string of events that would lead to him dying in Parry Sound – I asked outright what had happened between him and my mother. We were playing rummy, just about the only game we ever played. He no longer really understood some of the rules, but going through the motions was one of the few things still available to him. When I did get the question out, his explanation, like so much about him over the years, was disappointingly simple, one word, the name of the woman he'd left my mother for. She was quite a bit younger than my dad – like all the women that came after my mother – and until just recently I saw her only through the merciless eyes of a ten-year-old. What I see now is a young woman being taken in by my father's seemliness – man of the world, top of his game – when what she'd really attached herself to was someone who was never going to be much help with anything.

He had four marriages in the end, the last an arrangement that slowly made its way to the altar. They were together for about two and a half decades – almost as long as he lasted with my mother – and to my surprise, I was happy for them. They seemed genuinely suited to one another in a modest, cosy, happily-ever-after sort of way. It probably helped that my father was entering the latter stages of his career flight path. Gone, perhaps, was some of the old dazzle, and maybe he knew it and was able to recognize that here for once was someone who seemed to be coming to him without expecting much more than companionship – and that this was OK. But I'll say it straight up. To me it always felt that what lay at the bottom of them seeing eye-to-eye was that they were both essentially kids strutting about in adult-sized bodies.

Their house was a fairy-tale-ish thing with gingerbread trimmings, halfway up a quiet one-way street in one of Toronto's older suburbs. It had the mandatory four-car garage – something my father always needed, owing to his predilection for classic British sports cars. The house itself was crammed with a mix of antiques and comfortable places to sit. And while there was never a whole lot of room to move around, for years whoever could make it would squeeze themselves into his place on New Year's Day for a sort of after-the-fact potluck Davies family Christmas dinner. It was his wife who pretty much made it happen, and whatever heart there was, whatever effort went into making my father appear at all like a family man, you could be sure it was her that was behind it. The yearly birthday cards for my kids, these were her as well. It pretty much stopped there, but it was something.

It all went sour towards the end. Just weeks after my father's ninetieth birthday he wound up in hospital. His physical and mental capacities were judged to have fallen below the line that allows for much independence. It quickly became clear that the two of them had never seriously considered the possibility that a day like this might come.

I went to visit him a few times after he went back home, driving in from Peterborough, where I'd moved with my small family more than a decade earlier. I went despite not really wanting to be there. One time I took him out for a drive. We wound up at Cherry Beach. I'd brought some lunch for us to share, but when my father saw there was a food truck he became fixated on the idea of a hot dog – so I got him one.

Over the years I made some effort when it came to finding gifts for my father. For his helmet collection there was a Persian lamb RCMP wedge cap; another time it was a Russian tank driver's helmet I came across in Peshawar. And once I found him a pin that was described to me as the pin that was worn by those who were unable to serve in the Second World War, the war my father missed because of a heart murmur. He'd mentioned more than once the dirty looks he got at the time, a seemingly able-bodied young man not in uniform. This pin, had he had one, would have made it clear to others that he'd *tried* to sign up, tried but was unable to go. So when I came across one, I bought it. It was meant to say, 'Look. I've been listening.' He looked and said, 'No, that's not it.'

But a hot dog. In the end, this was the thing. For the short span remaining to him he mentioned that Cherry Beach hot dog with unrestrained enthusiasm every time I saw him. I can still picture that day – the sun, the row of trees, the beach stretched out behind us, me walking across the dusty parking lot to the food truck, and back again – then watching him, seated in the passenger seat of my Dodge Caravan, absolutely *devouring* that thing. Me, the son who bought him a hot dog. And it's just possible I'm oversimplifying both the undercurrents and superficialities of our relationship by bringing it down to this – to a hot dog. But when I think of the times he took me travelling in the decade after my parents' divorce, trips to Europe that were meant to somehow make up for him being almost completely absent the rest of the time, I begin to understand the importance of the hot dog and the joy it brought him. The ungilded cheapness of it embodied the near-perfect irony needed to balance out the equation between us. Four trips to Europe = one hot dog. Revealing – damning – funny.

4

And then he died. He fell in his driveway, wound up in one hospital and then another, and eventually one of my sisters offered to take him in. He was ferried up to her cottage, since it was summer and that was where she always spent it.

The timing was spectacular. It just so happened we were all about to congregate there – all his children, and a great many of his grandchildren and great-grandchildren. There was something unreal about that time at the cottage, that so many of us should have been there all at once, like the slow exhale of a this-is-your-life dream sequence from a movie. Or perhaps more accurately, this-was-*not*-your-life, since for decades he'd so rarely had much to do with any of our lives.

After a few days we all began to trickle home, and my father remained at the cottage. He had another fall and was taken to hospital in Parry Sound where he wound up in the ICU for a week, after which it was deemed that any further treatment would be strictly palliative. But it never came to that. He died while being transferred out of the ICU.

As with so many of the important things in my life, for what followed all I had to do, pretty much, was show up. The funeral amounted to little more than a burial, the ashes arriving at the cemetery in a hat tin that had belonged to my father, a nod to the foreverness of his fascination with head-wear. And whoever wanted to was encouraged to bring something to toss in with the ashes, tokens to accompany his memory on whatever path it would take from there. I knew exactly what to bring. In 1971 my father took me to an amusement park called Fantasy Island. It rained for much of the day and they closed the park. We were given rain checks, two of them, good for a return visit anytime that year. They wound up in my care, and for forty-five years they stayed in a chocolate box full of childhood keepsakes. When we got to the cemetery I flipped those rain checks into the hat tin with the ashes, whispering that it was his turn to hold on to them.

The following day we went to my father's house to pick up the things set aside in his will for his children and grandchildren. There were shelves filled with the militaria he'd collected, helmets mostly, the oldest dating back to the English Civil War. There were a few family mementos, as well as half a century's worth of artwork – his artwork. Magazine illustrations, fashion advertisements, ads for booze and cigarettes and cars, dozens of nudes, paint-ings of ships and airplanes, illustrations for company reports and a great many book covers. For one publisher alone he did somewhere in the neigh-bourhood of five hundred of these. When I was younger he'd occasionally have me model for him. Sometimes this happened on my way home from school, when I'd stop by his studio to collect my mother's alimony cheque. He'd have me pose a few different ways and take photos, since it was largely these he worked from. The earliest I remember, I stood in for Oliver Twist. In the very last I was a Greek god for the cover of a romance novel. He used both me and my wife for that one, though from the painting you'd never guess it was me. Not much of a Greek god, I suppose. My wife, though – in the cover illustration she's fairly identifiable. But my father liked the way she looked – and said so. Nice cheekbones. He was always saying things like this, judgements that left the impression that appearances were somehow central

Rosie and Ruby

RUBY EASTWOOD

The girls' mothers had met at the school gates in the first week of September. They had noticed each other on the first day, because both had turned up a bit late and disorganized. Both were single mothers and both tended to imagine that the other parents were in possession of a manual that they would neither talk about nor share.

Rosie and Ruby's mothers were not otherwise similar, and would probably not have been friends in any other context. Rosie's mother lived in a spacious flat that had once been a warehouse. She had bought it cheaply when she first arrived in Dublin in the '90s, before the loft aesthetic became widely desirable. She picked up work when she needed to, asking around among the friends she had made when she worked in the fashion industry, and they were always happy to hire her to help out with a campaign or a set for some small film. Her taste was known to be impeccable.

Ruby's mother had never had the time to think about taste. She had grown up with five brawling brothers in a council house, and had become pregnant by accident when she was too young. Even if she had wanted to ascertain who the father was, she knew it wouldn't have made any material difference. When she wasn't working she was studying for a psychology degree, her hair falling out of its haphazard bun.

Rosie's mother, noticing that Ruby was often the last to be picked up from school at the end of the day, started taking the girls home for playdates. Rosie and Ruby amused each other, running around in their own little world, and in the meantime she could get on with her own stuff. Ruby's mother would come over to the house and look after both girls on her days off. The girls were so similar, with their soft golden curls and rounded features, pink at the cheeks and fingertips. Watching them play, Ruby's mother would think of a lecture she had heard on Lacan's mirror stage. The girls did not quite understand where one began and the other ended. If Rosie hit Ruby and Ruby cried, Rosie would cry too, feeling the sting on her own cheek. They existed in a happy symbiosis.

Rosie's mother's bathroom was where the girls were inducted into the mysteries of womanhood. She had jewellery cases with sliding panels, hidden compartments, unfolding mirrors. She had toolboxes with tiny scissors and scrapers and files, and a million shades of nail polish, and pink foam pads with crenellations to go between the toes while the paint dried. She had face masks to dry out the skin and things to rub on after to rehydrate it, tweezers to get rid of eyebrows and special pencils to draw them back on again. Her world was marvellous to the girls. It was all so absurd, so poetic. Silk and cashmere, palo santo, cologne. She had dined in foreign countries, had entered rooms and struck fear and love into the hearts of strangers.

Rosie and Ruby loved to watch her as she prepared to go out in the evenings. They would sit on the rim of the bath and she would chat to them while she wound bits of hair around a heated tong, tendrils of steam rising. She would comment on the things she was doing, explaining that it was necessary to brush out the curls after you had finished with the tong, in order to make the waves appear natural and effortless. It struck the girls as strange that looking effortless was far more difficult and time-consuming than looking like you had made an effort, but they accepted it because it was in keeping with the paradoxical nature of her world.

Sometimes, Rosie's mother would use these bathroom sessions to warn them about going out at night. Her words sounded more like grim prophecy than motherly advice – they weren't yet old enough to even think about going out at night – and sometimes it seemed like she wasn't talking to them at all. Her advice was always the same. When you go into the dark, don't go alone, go in numbers. If you happen to be separated, don't take any short-cuts, stay on the bright streets. Remember that the heel of your shoe is a weapon. If you happen to be wearing flats, carry your keys in your fist with the sharp edge extended out. Don't rely on strength, think strategy. The soft places are at the nape of the neck, the meeting of the ribs, the eye socket, the groin. Stay alert to the sounds around you, listen for footsteps, and watch for shadows cast in front of you by the streetlamps. Leaving your napkin on top of your drink may help your peace of mind but it's a flimsy precaution. There's a special type of nail polish that will change colour when exposed to certain chemicals, but you may as well spare yourself the expense by taking your drink with you to the bathroom.

The picture she presented of womanhood was confusing to the girls, flitting as it did between lighthearted makeup tips and dystopian visions of the city at night, of violence and bloodshed. When she finally set out into the night it was always alone, contrary to her own instructions, and she did not seem scared. She was also apparently unconcerned about leaving the girls to look after themselves. She called out her goodbye as a kind of afterthought before the door clicked shut behind her, as if the other world she was rushing into was already more real to her than the one inside the house. The girls would go to the window in Rosie's room and watch her walk down the street, imagining where she might be going.

Once, there had been a man waiting for her. He was standing on the other side of the street, visible in the lamplight, and the girls debated whether or not he was handsome, though their view was partially obscured by the branches of a tree. When the couple started walking away, Rosie's mother's shoe fell off, and the man bent to pick it up. He kneeled in front of her, placing one of her feet on his knee and sliding the shoe back on. It was like something out of a fairy tale: she was looking down, hair falling over her face, and he was kneeling, head bowed, adjusting the strap around her ankle. Though they never spoke of it again, the image remained in both girls' minds for a long time after. This, they knew, was what it meant to be beautiful.

What they wished for with increasing fervour over the years was beauty that had the quality of truth: simple and irrefutable. They wondered if it was too late for the fairy godmother to come bursting through the doors bearing that gift, and knew that they would accept it immediately, without worrying what curse might come with it.

Of the two, Rosie was more affected by images of fantasy and fairy tale. She wanted to grow up to be like the women in the Pre-Raphaelite paintings reproduced on postcards in her house: Ophelia floating like a petal on the murky river water, Persephone coming out of the shadows with a pomegranate, Titania circled by glowing fairies in a dark forest. She could stare forever at the swan-like women, their mournful necks, the silk folds of their robes. They were painted against darkness so that their beauty shone out all the more startlingly. She wanted to slip out of the badly lit modern world and into those paintings, into Arthurian castles and mythical forests. Most of all she wanted to slip into the bodies of those women, because she knew that real beauty is never shallow, it confers destiny and depth, it places you forever at the centre of the composition, casting off light, dark branches bending around you.

When adolescence came it slid between the girls like a blade, making them aware of their new edges. For the first time they saw themselves from outside. Their bodies changed and diverged. Ruby's hair darkened while Rosie's stayed fair. Rosie's breasts grew first, at a rate that worried her. Delicate silvery stretch marks appeared on their tender undersides and on her hips and thighs. She felt betrayed by this sudden excess of flesh she had not asked for and did not know how to get rid of. Rosie's mother had been known throughout the girls' childhood to use the word 'fat' not only in the sense most people use it, but also in a broader, more abstract way to denote certain types of behaviour. If you asked for seconds, or ate the crust on your slice of pizza, you were *being fat*. Fatness lurked like a monster in all people, even the thinnest, and would come out to ravage you if you let it. There was something levelling in the thought that everyone, even Kate Moss and Bella Hadid, could *be fat*. And if fatness was the monster stalking everyone, then it was only the most virtuous who never let the monster in.

For a while, when Rosie had stopped eating, she looked like her mother. After six months of looking like her mother, her period stopped. She adopted a diet of dark chocolate and parmesan. The foods were so dense, so rich, that it would be sickening to eat enough of them in a day to meet a normal caloric intake. Rosie's new diet was representative of something Ruby had always admired about her friend, a certain combination of austerity and decadence. It marked her out as grown up and therefore glamorous.

The next phase of Rosie's recovery involved making elaborate cakes for others. She would spend hours watching YouTube videos of cake being cut and iced to resemble flowers and mushrooms and Disney princesses. Once she had done her initial research, she would labour over different types of icing, setting them out on the kitchen table in a colour gradient. The cakes she made always looked beautiful and tasted awful. She would plunge her knife into them with real spite and serve the pieces with whipped cream. Then she would watch Ruby as she tried her first spoonful. Do you like it, she would ask, her eyes very bright, very large in her face. Have another piece, she would say. She never indulged in a second helping of anything, and always made a point of not finishing what was on her plate.

Ruby knew that Rosie's eating habits were unhealthy, but she couldn't help admiring her friend's new sinuous grace. She looked artistic like this, Ruby thought. Or perhaps it was more that she had gained the status of an art *object*, flesh whittled away to reveal the sculptural contours of her bones. Her thinness conveyed expensiveness and seriousness, like a Giacometti. Ruby had attempted on various occasions to go a whole day without eating, but always buckled around lunchtime. On other occasions, she had tried to put her fingers down her throat, and once had succeeded in bringing up a whole meal. Afterwards when she sat by the toilet bowl, trembling, her vision slightly bleached, she had felt her own ridiculousness so powerfully she never attempted to do it again.

It was not just her lack of discipline that spared her. Her mother was not Rosie's mother. When she returned home to oven chips and broccoli, to her mother's tired warmth, she was always dismayed by the shabbiness of her life and at the same time grateful. After her shower, her mother would dry and plait her hair, and they would fall asleep together.

There was a scene in one of Ruby's favourite films, *The Pursuit of Love*, in which Fanny's mother advises her to ditch her better-looking friend Linda. As Fanny's mother points out, the girls' friendship will have the effect of exaggerating Linda's beauty while making Fanny's deficiencies evident to everyone. Ruby knew, rationally, that she was not fat, but sometimes when she stood next to Rosie, with her thin wrists and prominent collarbones, she would feel herself to be too solid, and thus worldly and common, and she would wonder whether everyone else could see it too.

It was not nice to think that way, but the more she tried to suppress it in herself the more she saw it playing out in the world around her. She saw it in old portraits, when high-class ladies posed with their ugly lapdogs. She saw it in weddings, when the bride would dress all her female friends in shapeless satin sacks. It was the essential premise of most of her favourite films, set in American high schools. Popular girls want friends who are pretty enough to ensure that they are viewed firmly within the category of hot girls, but not so good-looking that their own attractiveness is threatened. Maintaining that tension is the job of the mean girl, who must mould the appearances of her friends so that they reflect her image weakly, highlighting the perfection of the original.

Rosie and Ruby came to an unspoken agreement with regards to this problem. They fabricated artificial differences between themselves. If one of them laid claim to a song, a style, a film, the other knew to back away from it. They decided their respective cocktails before they had ever tried them: Rosie was a French sidecar, Ruby was a gin martini. Rosie was long dresses and bare feet, Manet, Marianne Faithfull, Gucci Bloom, Sofia Coppola. Ruby was dark roots and fur coats, New Wave, Joan Didion, menthol filters, David Lynch. They hoped that by arranging their likes and dislikes, they would create a constellation that was unique. They wanted very badly to be unique, not realizing that in that respect they were exactly like everybody else.

They posted compulsively, talked about things they didn't understand, and viewed their every experience in terms of aesthetics. They had a Spotify playlist for every imaginable state of mind. They were nostalgic and naively romantic. They were both playing at the same game, and the rules had been set long before they were born.

When they started going to parties, they would steal Rosie's mum's makeup box from her bathroom and sneak it into Rosie's room. They would sit on the bed with lots of cotton swabs around them and practise the flicks at the corners of their eyes until they were perfectly symmetrical, then stare into the mirror at their new, feline features. They would do their lips to look like the girls who popped up on their screen when they were trying to stream a film for free: a dark line drawn over the lip line, fading to a lighter shade at the centre, gloss layered on top like an overripe cherry, or bubblegum blown to bursting point.

They often reminded each other of the story a girl in school had told them about her older sister, who had swallowed a worm in a pill on purpose, so that she could carry on eating and lose weight. She had ordered it online from some sketchy Swiss doctor. He posted videos advertising his products in which he would swear on his mother's life that the worm method was completely safe.

The idea was wonderful. The worm inside the girl would grow fat while she grew thinner. One day in the toilet at school she had to pull the whole dead length of it out of her body, a bloody business that took ages. It had grown so much it had a face that was visible. Worms don't have eyes but they do have mouths. The girl had to break up with her boyfriend, who couldn't figure out what had gone wrong. She only told her little sister, who was sworn to secrecy, but what child can keep a secret so strange, so vile?

These were the stories they repeated to themselves in the hours while they readied themselves for the party. Once their makeup was done, they would play around with every permutation of an outfit, swapping hoop earrings for pearl-drops, putting their hair up in a heap and then down again, trying socks on under heels like Courtney Love and losing courage at the last moment, running back up the stairs to take them off, to rub red lipstick off with toilet roll. It was only many years later, long after they had lost contact, that Rosie and Ruby would understand that the most sacred moments of their girlhood had been before the parties, when they would drink cranberry juice and vodka and listen to music out of tinny phone speakers in Rosie's room. They couldn't remember a single conversation they had had at any of those parties, or even the names of the boys who had pressed against them in the dark with their bulging trousers. All those fumblings, which had seemed so important at the time, were forgotten. Forgotten too were the small betrayals and slights that had left them howling in the corner of some house party or other. Instead, what they remembered was the warm circle of lamplight by Rosie's bed, the branches rattling at the window, and the feeling of anticipation twisting inside them like a fish on a hook while the whole, unknown expanse of their lives beckoned from beyond the room.

The work van

JUSTINE SWEENEY

The work van is gone, so Dad picks me up in a borrowed Beetle. He hands
me a lollipop and sucks on one himself, nipping through West Belfast traffic.

'How was camogie?'

'Alright. Pauline tackling dirty again.'

'Hmm.'

'Does what she wants and gets away with it.'

'Don't let her annoy you,' he replies, but his attention has slipped into the
distance. He is keeping space between us and the army jeep he's spotted up
ahead.

The car stinks. Last week when he got it, Dad wiped down the dashboard
and trims, but old smoke has been woven into the upholstery fabric for too
many years.

At a red light, we stop a car-length behind the jeep. The rear doors are
fixed open. Four soldiers sit crammed in, two facing two on moulded side
benches. They love to drive around like this when there's nothing happening.

I wind the window crank, but it only gives an inch. The radio is bust too.
Dad had Queen in the tape deck of the work van. He'd sing and thump and
thrash and poke me in the side until I gave in and added air guitar to the
mix. Now, idling in the Beetle, his lolly stick stands alert between fingers
clenched on the wheel.

One of the soldiers swings around to face us. He's skinny in the face, but
a bulletproof vest pads out his body and camouflage combats are puffed until
they gather into black boots. Hoisting a rifle from his lap, he presses it
against his shoulder, points it at my father and tilts his head to the side, one
eye closed and the other peeping through the target finder.

The light goes green. They don't move off. Skinny swipes his rifle so it's pointing at me now. Holding it there, he looks at my father and licks his lips while the others shake from laughing.

I look down. We shouldn't even be in this Beetle, with the leather all worn off the gear stick, exposing rough patches of dried-out glue on a plastic knob that was never supposed to be seen by anyone.

Last month when the RA men came, I opened the door to them, but my grandmother came running out: 'You're not taking the van.'

'Calm yourself, missis,' one of them said.

'He's not in. Keys aren't here.'

One of the men, pushing my grandmother against the open front door, lifted keys from the hall table: 'This them?'

'He'll get sacked. You're supposed to be on our side but you're no better than the Brits.'

At that he swung and shoved her, making the door knocker lift and bang above her head. 'You know, luv, a wee bit of thanks wouldn't go amiss.'

Finally the army jeep pulls away. Dad jerks the gearstick into first, but the Beetle conks out and the engine floods. He flings his lollipop against the dashboard, and all I can think of is the stolen work van screeching off into the night.

Darina Laracy's wars

NIAMH CULLEN

In the spring of 1940, after graduating from the Sorbonne with an MA in history, Darina Laracy boarded a train bound for Italy. Europe was at war, and home was in Dublin. But the man who wanted to marry her, Carlo Macchi, was in Milan. Darina and Carlo had met in the summer of 1935 as students on a German-language course in Freiburg. They kept in touch afterwards by letter, and Darina visited Milan in 1938. Carlo had an apartment with five rooms, a servant, and a governess lined up for the children he hoped they'd have. But Darina had been putting him off for months before she travelled to Milan. She left her winter clothes in Paris, which may suggest that she didn't intend to be gone too long.

In Milan, Darina finally agreed to marry Carlo. They went to Rome and on 3 May presented at the Irish legation to post their marriage banns. They were still together in Rome when Hitler invaded France on 10 May. But when Carlo returned to Milan, Darina remained in Rome.

On 10 June, Mussolini declared war on Britain and France, and Italy's borders closed. Much later, Darina described this as a sudden shock to her plans, leaving her stranded in Italy with no possibility of return to Paris: in this version of events, the engagement did not figure. In any case, it is clear that Rome – not Milan – was where she wanted to be, and Carlo would have to be satisfied with visiting her there. It appears she began to seek work before the borders closed, and she quickly found a job as an assistant to John Whitaker, a correspondent for the *New York Herald Tribune* and the *Chicago Daily News*.

In a series of interviews she gave much later, when in her eighties, Darina spoke of the interests and beliefs that had put her on this unusual trajectory. She had, she said, pasted a photograph of Giacomo Matteotti, the Italian socialist politician murdered by fascists in 1924, on the wall of her bedroom in the Laracy home in Rathgar. Young Irish women were expected to settle down and marry after their studies, but Darina wanted, more than anything else, to travel. She claimed to have been frustrated by the apathy of her fellow UCD students towards the worsening political situation in Europe. After graduating with BA in history and politics from UCD in 1938, she was awarded a 'travelling scholarship' from the National University of Ireland to undertake postgraduate study in Paris. But even in Paris, she was impatient to move on. She tried to volunteer for the Spanish Republic on arrival, but was turned down, since she had no relevant skills. It is difficult in retrospect to separate Darina's desire to fight fascism – professed in later life – from her evident thirst for travel and adventure. But for a woman university graduate, working for the press might have seemed the best way to contribute to the fight against fascism, or at least tell the truth about it. John Whitaker was no anti-fascist himself, having been awarded the Croce di Guerra (War Cross) for his coverage of the Italian invasion of Ethiopia in 1936, although by 1940 his articles were becoming more critical of the regime.

Darina took lodgings in the attic room of an elegant apartment building just off Via Veneto: a neighbourhood of embassies, government ministries and fashionable hotels and cafés. She passed her days between the newspaper offices and press briefings at the Ministry for Foreign Affairs, where she claimed to have gained a reputation for asking hard-hitting questions. Evenings were spent at glamorous parties with princes and diplomats, interspersed with quieter gatherings at Whitaker's apartment, where guests drank Frascati wine and listened to classical records. 'I found it simply amusing to sally forth from my attic to an embassy reception,' she wrote in a letter describing this period, 'utterly unperturbed by the fact of being devoid of diamonds; to come home from a palace and climb up my backstairs to be deposited by the office by a king's son etc.'

Darina lived and worked in the small web of steep, wide streets between

Termini Station and the Spanish Steps, where Rome's international residents congregated. Those who remained in the wartime city were mainly journalists, and diplomats representing those friendly or neutral nations, like Ireland and (until December 1941) the US, that had not suspended their embassies. Rome was still somewhat insulated from the war: there were no bombs falling, nor were there yet any food shortages. The work 'sucked one's blood', Darina wrote in a long letter home in July 1942, but she dealt with the stress by socializing. During her first six months, she explained, she found herself 'so worn out by politics in the evening at 8.30 or 9pm, whenever the Job was technically finished for the day (actually it never finished) my very superficial reaction was to stay in company and go to the most elegant places in Rome'.

She might have been aware by late 1940 that she was being tracked by the fascist secret police (OVRA), who opened a file on her that September, noting her work for Whitaker and Carlo's regular visits to Rome. In October, 'into this more or less Eden crawled the serpent', as she put it in a letter she wrote the following year. Coming out of a press conference one day, she told the interviewer, she noticed that she was being followed by a shifty-looking man. The man stopped to ask if she would like a more glamorous and better-paid job: a job that would allow her to travel. She realized immediately what sort of work he meant and told him she wasn't interested in being a spy. He wouldn't take no for an answer. 'He was outside my front door every day and went everywhere I did', displaying wads of dollars as a crude temptation, she recalled.* Finally, Darina became exasperated and asked to speak to his superior. She received a phone call from a man called Rossetti, who spoke Italian with a German accent. Darina agreed to meet him in a nearby bar to set things straight. 'Please, can you get rid of this annoyance,' she recalled saying to him. 'In any case, I will never work as a spy for you. I won't spy for anyone, but if I had to do it, I'd do it for the other side.'

Darina concluded that Rossetti was attached to the Gestapo, which was operating unofficially in Italy at this time. She recalled that she met him sev-

*The translations of quotations from the interviews with Darina – published in a 2005 book titled Colloqui, edited by Michele Dorigatti and Maffino Maghenzani – and from the police reports, are my own.

eral more times in an effort to put him off for good. Why meet him at all? Per Darina's recollection in the late interviews, it was obvious from the outset what the offers of work were about. But in the July 1942 letter to her parents, she wrote that when these 'manoeuvres' began, she had 'no idea of their significance'. This version of events is far more plausible. The conflict in Darina's recollections may give us doubts about other elements of the story she told late in life about her interactions with Rossetti. In her account, he grew impatient, insisting that everyone had their price. 'If you work with us for just a few months,' she recalled him saying, 'you'll have enough money to keep yourself in diamonds and furs for the rest of your life.' We know you are a spy already, he added – a common accusation thrown at journalists – so why not do it for us too? Darina claimed that when she told Rossetti that she had no price, he mentioned Carlo, suggesting that the Italian authorities had exchanged information with the German embassy. Within a fortnight, something terrible will happen to him, Rossetti told her.

In one of the late interviews, Darina said that she tried to warn Carlo, but that he didn't take the threat seriously. A keen Alpine climber who was well known in mountaineering circles, he set off soon afterwards, with two companions, to tackle Monte Rosa: the second highest of the Alps, on the border between Italy and Switzerland. He had attempted it three times previously but was thwarted each time by poor weather. Darina claimed that Carlo's companions cut his rope as they made their descent, abandoning his body on the slope. Nobody else suspected foul play, although in her recollection locals wondered about the conduct of two mountaineers who would abandon a companion in difficulty. Carlo Macchi died on 1 March 1941, at the age of twenty-seven.

In Darina's account, this terrible event was followed by a sinister phone call from Rossetti: 'Now do you realize we were serious?' He seemed to hope that the murder of her fiancé would make her see sense and come on board as a spy. It won't be like you are imagining from the films, he said. All you will have to do is pass little scraps of paper back and forth.

Darina's version of events is impossible to verify, and seems hard to credit. Would the Gestapo have used such elaborate measures, making a murder seem like a mountaineering accident, purely in order to convince someone to spy for them? A short article in the Milan newspaper *Corriere della Sera*, dated 5 March 1941, records the accidental death of Carlo Macchi, survived by his mother and by two brothers serving at the front. There is no mention of his fiancée, Darina Laracy. The two men who went up Monte Rosa with him are named. One of them, Bruno Ceschina, was from a well-known Milan industrialist family who lived near Carlo, and the two were members of the same mountaineering club. Ceschina seems an unlikely Gestapo agent. (According to a later article, Ceschina himself died in a similar accident in September 1945.)

We will never know exactly what passed between Darina and Rossetti. Darina's police file contains a memo from the Roman police headquarters to the Ministry of War, dated 22 March 1941, which makes the ambiguous claim that she 'belonged to the German secret service, although they were not able to make use of her services'. As we shall see, Darina had a motivation, late in life, to exaggerate the degree to which she had been at odds with, and victimized by, the fascists. But her belief that the Gestapo was involved in Carlo's death was sincere – as is evident from her July 1942 letter to her parents. There, she described Carlo's death as an 'assassination' and wrote of her feeling that she 'had been the cause of it'.

Although the interviews Darina gave in her eighties have the feel of an adventure story, emphasizing how she stood up to the Gestapo, the letters she wrote home reveal a quieter story of grief and fear. In the July 1942 letter, she wrote that after Carlo's funeral in Milan, 'I returned to Rome like a squeezed lemon, absolutely nothing left inside: total collapse of everything. […] I worked absolutely as usual, like a machine. In fact I wanted to work all the time. […] I didn't want time to think about anything.' It was also around this time that John Whitaker, her boss at the *New York Herald Tribune*, was expelled from Italy for his mounting criticism of the regime. Darina stayed on at the newspaper working for his successor, Allen Raymond, while taking an extra job at the Irish legation. 'I gave up seeing everyone and went nowhere. [...] I became completely indifferent to everything that happened to me. There was an abyss between my inward feelings, mostly suffocated despair and Sahara emptiness, and my outward behaviour [...] I could if necessary have gone to a ball on the day of C.'s funeral, the mechanical act of dancing would have had nothing to do with what I felt.'

At the same time, the Italian authorities were closing in on Darina. The 22 March 1941 police memo advised that 'taking account of the current state of war, the harmful actions of this foreign woman in Italy, and the danger that she represents for ability, charm, intelligence and the possibility of infiltration at many levels, especially now that she is in the service of the journalist Allen Raymond, we propose her expulsion from the Italian kingdom.' In one of the late interviews, Darina remarked: 'I've always thought that Italian attitudes towards women are a little extreme.'

In late April or early May, the police knocked on Darina's door in Rome. She was charged with the vague crime of 'suspected espionage' and given a week to leave Italy. She was convinced that this, too, was the Gestapo's doing, although given Whitaker's recent expulsion and the close watch that the OVRA kept on Allen Raymond, the Italian authorities may not have needed much further prompting to give the order. A week was not enough time to get the necessary transit visas to travel through Europe, and Darina approached the Irish legation to plead for more time. She also made use of her society contacts – among them a Polish emigré prince – in order to secure the travel documents.

'I discovered in the last few weeks', she wrote in her July 1942 letter to her parents, 'how many friends I had and how much I loved the beastly country, but on the other hand the atmosphere of terror, spying and persecution was such that I could hardly wait to get out, it was undermining everyone's nerves.' In mid-June 1941, having secured a visa to enter Switzerland, Darina took the train northwards. She stopped briefly in Milan to visit the Macchi family before crossing the border into Swiss territory.

2

Darina went first to the capital, Berne, where she stayed for a few months. She sought work at the British legation, which was also becoming the base of British wartime intelligence in Europe, hoping to be transferred to London. She socialized and networked intensely, although she soon tired of the claustrophobia and frivolity of diplomatic life in a neutral capital. Vague offers of work in Britain or Berne came to nothing. In November 1941, she moved to Zürich. She first took lodgings beside Lake Zürich before moving to another rented room in the hills above the city. She kept this address for two years until she moved away from Zürich for good.

Her visa did not allow her to work, and she began to pass her time reading and writing at the Museumgesellschaft library, where, decades earlier, James Joyce had spent many hours working on *Ulysses*. It was here that she had a chance meeting with the Italian writer Ignazio Silone. A founding member of the Italian Communist Party, Silone had been expelled by the party for going against Stalin in 1931. Well known across Europe in the 1930s for his best-selling novel *Fontamara*, a fictional exposé of fascism in rural Italy, he had been living in political exile in Switzerland for over a decade.

Darina had read her father's copy of *Fontamara* as a teenager in Dublin. She was not impressed by Silone – twenty years her senior – on their first meeting. But he persisted, and in their conversations she came to find the intellectual stimulation that she craved. The relationship was not at first a romantic one – 'I have neither the desire not the capacity to repeat the performance of being "madly" in love with anyone,' she wrote to her parents in July 1942. 'I still am with Carlo and feel too old for the repetition of such an élan.' But over the course of 1942, the relationship became more intimate.

In June 1942 Darina was held by the Swiss police for several days after a suitcase she left behind in Berne railway station awakened the suspicions that had followed Darina from Rome to Berne and Zürich: that she was a foreign spy. (A job offer from the Red Cross had been rescinded because of the same suspicions.) In a letter written a few weeks afterwards, she regaled her parents with the story of her arrest in spirited tones, as if she had found the episode a great amusement. When the police arrived at her lodgings early in the morning, Darina was still in bed. She dressed slowly, she wrote, 'just to spite them. It was warm, I wore a summer dress, no coat, gloves, sunglasses.' Her attitude, throughout the three days of interrogation, 'was one of cold British-empire disdain', a comment perhaps designed to impress her father, a decorated British army veteran turned civil servant, or her mother, the daughter of an RIC officer. 'In a way I rather enjoyed it,' she added, 'it was like being at the theatre.' In her own telling, Darina convinced the Swiss police of her innocence, impressing them with her eloquence, wit and quick thinking. The records indicate that some intervention was also made on her behalf by the Irish legation. On her release, the Swiss police shook hands with her and swore to defend her reputation themselves from then on, before she hurried back to her lodgings for lunch and a bath.

The letter to her parents about this episode was passed on to Lorna Reynolds, Darina's friend from her student days at UCD, presumably after her family read it: I found it among Darina's later letters to Lorna, which are held at the University of Limerick library. Darina mentioned in the letter to her parents how she had realized with 'growing horror and bewilderment' that previous letters home had been intercepted before they left the continent, never arriving in Dublin. 'I have never ceased to write regularly,' she assured her parents.

Once the OVRA figured out the connection between Darina and Silone (he always went by Silone, a pseudonym), they began to watch Darina more assiduously and to intercept her correspondence. This explains the presence in Silone's police file of the two letters that Darina wrote to her family in Dublin in early 1943; I discovered them in the central state archive in Rome.

Darina began to write the first letter close to midnight on New Year's Eve 1942. She had just walked through a snowstorm to get back to her room, where she immediately crawled into bed to keep warm. A funicular went only part of the way to her lodgings in the hills above the city, and many of the streets were so steep that the only way up was through a series of narrow, step-lined laneways. There was no heating in her room, and snow had seeped into her worn-out shoes. All she had to keep warm was a cup of bad coffee and her memories of previous New Year's Eves in Dublin. 'I am wondering if you are waiting up to hear midnight strike,' she wrote. She had no wireless and her watch wasn't working properly. 'But if I knew the exact time, I could think: at home you are listening to the clock strike and saying, well it's 1943 and wishing each other happy new years – and I could imagine you.'

In this letter and in the second, written ten days later, Darina recalled her life in Rome and mused about her uncertain future. The writing was wry, witty and dramatic. Darina's days in Switzerland lacked the urgency and purpose of her Roman life, although she sought to fill them as best she could. She had no hope of fitting in there, she wrote: the Swiss were a 'homely people' and in staid Zürich 'my lipstick is a permanent scandal'. Still traumatized by Carlo's death and her expulsion from Rome, she drifted between grief, regret, guilt, and the desire to do something to change her life. News from home was like a familiar beacon to light her dull days. 'I adore letters from home so much, if you knew how much you would write oftener. I know my letters are erratic but I do try to tell you as much as I can, which I admit is not much. If only I could see you, I would tell you everything at once. I think with world conditions what they are, parents grow up faster than they used to and can be told more than formerly.'

They needn't imagine anything too scandalous, she hastened to add: lipstick aside, she led 'a monastic existence'. Still unable to work, Darina relied on the monthly subsidy her parents wired from Dublin. She wanted to contribute to the war effort and to make some proper money. Preferably both, but either would do. She was experimenting with short stories, although she was no longer sure if her real talent lay in writing. She did a stint as a governess and even fed pigs in exchange for Russian lessons, wondering if communism was where the future – for herself and Europe – lay. She had hoped at various points to leave Switzerland, although how, or what work she hoped to do, was unclear. She was probably taking the Russian lessons in the hope of being able to travel to Russia, although when or in what capacity was never clear. Perhaps she was not sure herself. She was still waiting, in that long winter of 1942–3, for her true calling to reveal itself.

Her relationship with Silone had deepened. They had long conversations most days, and when Darina was away from Zürich, Silone wrote to her daily. He acted as a mentor, critiquing her writing and introducing her to publishers. As he came to trust Darina, he also allowed her entry into the clandestine anti-fascist resistance. She began taking on some tasks for the Italian Socialist Party, whose Swiss branch was headed by Silone. The work was mundane – mainly translation and administrative work – but Darina was finally contributing to a cause that she believed in. She felt that Silone was helping her back to life after the trauma and shock of her final months in Rome. As she described it, it was as though she was 'beginning to recover consciousness after an anaesthetic'. At the same time, he irritated her. He was constantly fussing over her. He foisted complicated cold remedies on her and advised her to pray, although she was no longer a believer. She was beginning to find the endless letters and attention stifling. At times he reminded her of her mother.

That New Year's Eve, Darina was facing a decision. Silone had been arrested and imprisoned earlier that month. In a broadcast for the BBC, he had named himself as head of the Italian Socialist Party in Switzerland. This was deemed a breach of the conditions of Swiss neutrality, which did not allow any foreign political activity. He was held in prison for sixteen days before suffering a 'lung attack' – he suffered from tuberculosis – and being released on condition that he leave the canton of Zürich. In the small mountain resort of Davos, he planned to continue his resistance activities far from the Zürich police while receiving sanatorium treatment for his tuberculosis. He had asked Darina to accompany him, and she was uncertain what to do. She used her long letter, written over several days, to think it out on paper. When she began writing, she was resolute in her intention to leave Silone, although she realized it would be difficult. Their lives had become enmeshed, and she knew he would not easily let her leave. 'If you go,' he told her, 'I shall have to create a secret service to have news of you.' By the time she wrote her second letter, dated 10 January, she had made the decision to go to Davos with him.

It was not love that bound her to Silone, she continued to insist. The relationship was more one of mentor and student, or a chaste medieval friendship between monk and nun, as Darina put it, than a modern intimate partnership. She was convinced that by working with him, she might make a meaningful contribution to the war effort. This was what she had desired since she graduated in 1940.

'And yet although almost everything seems to be wrong about my being here now,' Darina wrote to her parents, 'nevertheless I am convinced that now at last it is right – "duty" is rather complex and I don't seem to be very dutiful towards you at the moment, but towards "society".' The most important consideration for Darina was that she didn't want to go home. She would settle for London, Paris, even Moscow, if she could not be in Rome, but the thought of returning to Rathgar was unbearable. Silone drove her 'cracked', but he was interesting, and life with him was filled with purpose. He was also her remaining link with Italy, and through him, there was the chance of return.

Darina did not begin her correspondence with her close college friend Lorna Reynolds until August 1944, soon after Rome was liberated from Nazi occupation and Darina and Silone were making plans to return there together. The letter, beginning an epistolary relationship that would stretch across decades, opened by explaining Darina's silence during the early war years. At first, her failure to write was due to 'frivolity and laziness', but 'since 1941 it was not that anymore; I would have given a lot to be able to write to you. [...] But I was in such an internal state that I couldn't write. I simply had nothing to say, nothing except possibly, "oh dear Lorna. The only sensible thing to do is to shoot oneself." I thought it better to save a stamp on that.' The one person who saved her from her 'utter despair' was her companion Ignazio Silone.

By the end of 1944, Darina and Silone were in Rome, and married. She was twenty-seven years old. The marriage was not a happy one. Silone was controlling and psychologically abusive, making it difficult for Darina to keep in touch with friends and pursue the writing career she planned. Instead she spent her time doing mundane translations in order to make money. Darina's letters to Lorna Reynolds, which resumed, after the 1944 letter, in 1948, often expressed the longing to leave her marriage – and Italy – although she stopped short of wishing to return to Ireland. Darina's ambitions for her post-war life, although never well defined, evolved from the desire to become a published writer to the simpler wish for a job that would afford her financial independence. Unhappy and frustrated, Darina drank too much and took lovers, even leaving Silone briefly in 1955 to live with an Indian poet in London. Her letters to Lorna stop abruptly in 1955, so it's not clear exactly when she returned to Silone. She dedicated the following two decades to translation, the management of her husband's affairs, and taking care of the ageing Silone until his death in 1978. In the interviews that the elderly Darina gave, she cast herself in the role of faithful wife and widow.

3

In the late 1990s, her story changed again when a collection of letters apparently written by Silone between 1919 and 1930 was found in the central state archive and brought to light in a book by historians Mauro Canali and Dario Biocca. The letters were addressed to to a Roman police prefect, Guido Bellone, who by 1926 had become Inspector-General of the Political Police. From 1921 Silone had been a leading member of the newly founded Italian Communist Party. The party had existed mostly in exile since Mussolini declared it illegal after coming to power in 1922. Now it emerged that during all this time Silone had been a police informer.

The news was explosive in Italy: Silone was an icon of anti-fascism. It was as if, as Martin Clark put it in the *London Review of Books*, 'Orwell were suddenly shown to have spent his time in Catalonia working for Franco'. Writing under the code name 'Silvestri', Silone had sent numerous letters to Bellone, giving information on his fellow communists in exile in Paris, Berlin, Moscow and Spain. Much of the information was generic – descriptions of party strategy and discussions – although he also gave names and details of movement, for example of comrades travelling under forged passports, possibly leading to arrests.

Silone was long dead when the letters came to light, and Darina had been a child when he wrote them. But it was she who was tasked with explaining and defending his legacy. Although Darina – like some scholars – initially protested that the letters were forgeries, she was forced to accept the veracity of at least some of them. The scandal caused her 'many sleepless nights', she admitted to Silone's biographer, Stanislao Pugliese. She suggested that

Silone may have written to Bellone in hope of helping his brother Romolo, who was arrested in 1928; but that does not explain why he had been writing to Bellone since 1919. (Any pull Silone may have had with the police did not save Romolo, who died in prison in 1932.) Darina also maintained that Silone never intended to hurt any of his fellow communists, and hinted at the possibility of his being a triple agent. People now don't understand what it was like to live through those times, Darina went on, in one of the late interviews. 'After all, I too was considered a spy by everyone: even by Silone when I first met him.' Writing to Pugliese, she added: 'There are "official" documents "proving" that I was a Nazi spy' – a reference to the March 1941 letter from the Ministry of War. 'I am still alive to explain the weird circumstances of this – Silone is not.' This desire to 'explain' was presumably behind the series of interviews she gave, starting in 1999, recalling her life with – and without – Silone.

In June 2022 I visited the Centro Studi Ignazio Silone, a research centre in Silone's home village of Pescina, in the Abruzzo countryside east of Rome. Darina helped to set up the centre, donating Silone's papers and belongings to the museum and library. It was here that I met a number of people who knew Darina in later life. She survived Silone by twenty-five years until her own death in 2003. In her later decades she completed her husband's final novel and catalogued his papers for future study. The elderly Darina continued to read in several languages and had opinions on everything. Darina hosted scholars, writers and public figures at her apartment in Rome.

Some of the people I met in Pescina were convinced that Darina had been an agent for British or US intelligence, or both, during the war. Silone himself had collaborated with both British intelligence and the OSS, the predecessor of the CIA, during the war. His work with British intelligence began before he met Darina, but it may have been she who initiated his contact with Allen Dulles, who headed the OSS in Switzerland, in early 1943: her former colleague at the *New York Herald Tribune* in Rome, Betty Parsons, was then working for Dulles. This relationship led to the first scandal about Silone's past when, in the 1960s, it emerged that the left-wing (but anti-communist) magazine he edited had received CIA funding.

The question that has come to interest me most is how, following the revelations in the 1990s, Darina had to rethink the story she told, in public and in private, about the life they shared. Their union always appeared to be one of political and intellectual collaboration, more than love and companionship. Now, was the anchor story of Silone's anti-fascism to be taken from her? The fact that Silone wrote the letters appears undeniable. Darina admitted in the interviews that Silone remained, in part, a mystery to her too, 'but it precisely this "mystery" that I want to respect, and I believe that I have, staying with him until the end and dedicating myself to his work'.

4

I left my desk at the Central State Archive for the final time in October 2022, gathering the rest of my belongings from my locker, and beginning my walk to the metro station. The archive is in the EUR district of Rome, which was planned as the site of the 1942 Universal Exposition (or 'world's fair'). Mussolini's intention was to use EUR as a global fascist showcase on what would be the twenty-year anniversary of the March on Rome that brought him to power in 1922. The war intervened and the 1942 exposition never happened. The district languished, unfinished, until the mid-1950s when some of the more monumental constructions – including the archive building – were completed. The district as a whole is designed on too great a scale for human life, with its endless lines of grey stone cut with the hazy skyline of heat, sunshine and exhaust fumes.

When Darina was writing from Zürich in the winter of 1942–3, the war seemed interminable, the whole continent under Nazi–fascist occupation.

During my trip to Rome, the hundred-year anniversary of the March on Rome came and went, the marking of it almost as low-key as the twenty-year anniversary in 1942. There was little mention of it in Italian politics or the media. It was only a few weeks since the Italian election that had resulted in the formation of a government whose largest party can trace its roots directly back to Mussolini's fascist party. Both the new prime minister, Giorgia Meloni, and her opponents were deliberately staying quiet, both sides afraid of what might happen if the ghost of 1922 was invoked.

On 27 October, two banners were erected on the pedestrian bridge beside the Colosseum, one invoking the memory of fascism and the other decrying it. Photographs were shared in newspapers and on social media, before the banners were removed. There was disquiet and uncertainty over what Meloni's government would bring. There was also the concern about an unusually warm autumn, after a blistering summer: north of Rome the river Po is fast drying up. In that moment, as I descended into the gloom and heat of the metro station, I thought of Darina in December 1942, poised between one life and another; stranded in an alien city and caught in a war that seemed like it would never end.

Notes on contributors

ROISIN AGNEW is working on a feature film and a collection of short stories.

NIAMH CULLEN'S most recent book is *Love, Honour and Jealousy: An Intimate History of the Italian Economic Miracle*. She is working on a book about Darina Laracy Silone and a novel.

JOE DAVIES is working on a collection of short stories.

RUBY EASTWOOD is working on a collection of short stories.

NICK HOLDSTOCK'S most recent book is *Quarantine*, a novel.

JANE LAVELLE is working on a collection of short stories. Her essay about her wedding in Karachi appeared in *Dublin Review* 69 (Winter 2017–18).

RICHARD LEA is working on a collection of short stories, and he is the editor of *Fictionable*.

JESS RAYMON is working on a novel.

JUSTINE SWEENEY is working on a novella.

subscribe to *the* Dublin Review

Four times a year, *The Dublin Review* publishes first-rate writing from Ireland and elsewhere – essays, memoir, criticism, travel, reportage and fiction – by world-class writers.

A year's subscription to *The Dublin Review* brings four issues to your mailbox for the same low price you'd pay in a bookshop. It also makes a wonderful gift – or four gifts!

Annual subscription rates:
Ireland: €34
Rest of world: €45 / UK£36 / US$60
Institutions add €15 / UK£13 / US$20

It is easy to subscribe to *The Dublin Review* via our website: www.thedublinreview.com.

If you don't wish to subscribe via www.thedublinreview.com, please send a cheque to The Dublin Review, P.O. Box 7948, Dublin 1, Ireland, making sure to supply your full address.